Famous Fathers

"We're two people who wouldn't have met under normal circumstances...

...stuck with each other for a short period of time, who probably won't see each other again." The thought pained Madison. She foolishly wished things could be different. All the things Ryan had done to make her comfortable, not to mention his gentleness with her daughter, had her softening to him.

Ryan studied her. "I know you're right—"

"Of course I'm right," Madison interrupted. She didn't want to argue or analyze this. Nor did she want him to see that she found him handsome enough, steady enough, courageous enough, interesting enough, that she'd risk what she had to if there was any chance of a future together.

As she moved to leave, he pulled her back. "This isn't over, Madison. Not by a long shot...."

★ ★ ★ ★ ★

TEXAS FAMILY TIES:
With bonds stronger than blood,
these Texans are about to discover the true
meaning of family, friendship...and love.

Dear Reader,

This month, Silhouette Romance unveils our newest promotion, VIRGIN BRIDES. This series, which celebrates first love, will feature original titles by some of Romance's best-loved stars, starting with perennial favorite Diana Palmer. In *The Princess Bride,* a feisty debutante sets her marriage sights on a hard-bitten, cynical cowboy. At first King Marshall resists, but when he realizes he may lose this innocent beauty—forever—he finds himself doing the unthinkable: proposing.

Stranded together in a secluded cabin, single mom and marked woman Madison Delaney finds comfort—and love—in *In Care of the Sheriff,* this month's FABULOUS FATHERS title, as well as the first book of Susan Meier's new miniseries, TEXAS FAMILY TIES. Donna Clayton's miniseries MOTHER & CHILD also debuts with *The Stand-by Significant Other.* A workaholic businesswoman accepts her teenage daughter's challenge to "get a life," but she quickly discovers that safe—but irresistibly sexy—suitor Ryan Shane is playing havoc with her heart.

In Laura Anthony's compelling new title, *Bride of a Texas Trueblood,* Deannie Hollis would do *anything* to win back her family homestead—even marry the son of her enemy. In Elizabeth Harbison's sassy story, *Two Brothers and a Bride,* diner waitress Joleen Wheeler finds herself falling for the black-sheep brother of her soon-to-be fiancé…. Finally, Martha Shields tells a heartwarming tale about a woman's quest for a haven and the strong, silent rancher who shows her that *Home is Where Hank is.*

In April and May, look for VIRGIN BRIDES titles by Elizabeth August and Annette Broadrick. And enjoy each and every emotional, heartwarming story to be found in a Silhouette Romance.

Regards,

Joan Marlow Golan

Joan Marlow Golan
Senior Editor Silhouette Books

Please address questions and book requests to:
Silhouette Reader Service
U.S.: 3010 Walden Ave., P.O. Box 1325, Buffalo, NY 14269
Canadian: P.O. Box 609, Fort Erie, Ont. L2A 5X3

IN CARE
OF THE SHERIFF

Susan Meier

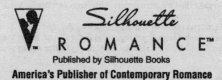

Silhouette
R O M A N C E™
Published by Silhouette Books
America's Publisher of Contemporary Romance

SILHOUETTE BOOKS

ISBN 0-373-19283-5

IN CARE OF THE SHERIFF

This edition published by arrangement with Harlequin Books S.A.

® and TM are trademarks of Harlequin Books S.A., used under license.
Trademarks indicated with ® are registered in the United States Patent
and Trademark Office, the Canadian Trade Marks Office and in other
countries.

Printed in U.S.A.

Books by Susan Meier

Silhouette Romance

Stand-in Mom #1022
Temporarily Hers #1109
Wife in Training #1184
Merry Christmas, Daddy #1192
**In Care of the Sheriff* #1283

Silhouette Desire

Take the Risk #567

*Texas Family Ties

SUSAN MEIER

has been an office manager, the division manager for a charitable organization and a columnist for a local newspaper. Presently, she holds a full-time job at a manufacturing company.

Even though her motto, The Harder You Work, The Luckier You Get, is taped to the wall of her office, Susan firmly believes you have to balance work and play. An avid reader and lousy golfer, she has learned to juggle the demands of her job and family while still pursuing her writing career and playing golf twice a week.

Fabulous Fathers

RYAN KELLY'S THOUGHTS ON FATHERHOOD:

When I was fifteen, I ran away from home. One thing I was sure of when I left was that I wasn't ever going to be a parent. My own parents left a great deal to be desired, and I figured that since I hadn't had good role models, I wasn't going to fare any better in the parenting department than they had.

But I got lucky. Though Angus MacFarland never officially adopted me, he intercepted me on my way to my fifth boarding school and helped me learn that life isn't merely about taking care of yourself, it is about taking care of those you love, too.

I guess the toughest thing to learn was that nobody's perfect—you can only do your best. And sometimes that means making compromises.

So, though my parents weren't exactly Ward and June Cleaver, I'm not worried about being a father anymore. When the time comes, I'll be ready.

I just hope I get that chance some day....

Prologue

Sixteen-year-old Ryan Kelly propelled Angus Mac-Farland's Bronco up the dry dirt road that led to Angus's ranch. The vehicle bounced and swayed, but Ryan easily controlled it, avoiding potholes and ruts while maintaining the high speed necessary to get him to the ranch as quickly as possible. Adrenaline surged through him. It was the first time in six weeks that he was happy. The first time in six weeks he felt free.

Reaching the house, he jammed his foot on the brake, and the Bronco careened to the left, then the right. Ryan grinned. Finally he'd found something fun in this godforsaken hellhole.

Angus opened the front door at the same time that Ryan jumped out of the Bronco.

"Jackson Wright collapsed," Ryan said, shielding his eyes from the bright Texas sun as he watched Angus jog down the three wooden steps of the wood plank porch. "Bucky told me to bring him back here to you."

"Damn it," Angus said, then he swiped his hand over his mouth.

Ryan suspected Angus knew today's problem with Jackson was alcohol induced and had very little to do with illness or injury, but he said nothing, waiting to see how Angus would handle this. Angus MacFarland, best friend of Ryan's father, was supposed to be a good man, a shining example after which Ryan was to pattern himself. Since he'd come to live with Angus six weeks ago, Ryan hadn't seen any evidence that Angus was the paragon Graham Kelly claimed him to be—though, Ryan had to admit, Angus hadn't really been tested before this.

Shifting his weight to his left foot, Ryan waited. Without a word, Angus strode to the Bronco and opened the door to the back seat where Jackson lay. From the look on Angus's face, Ryan knew the smell of whiskey had greeted him. Ryan held back a laugh. *Let's see how the paragon handles this one.*

"All right, we'll get him home," Angus said. He slammed the door on Jackson's prone form and reached for the passenger's side door handle. "You drive."

Ryan grinned, his respect for the old man climbing a notch, if only because he let Ryan drive. "You bet," Ryan said as he happily vaulted into the brand new Bronco. But Ryan's good humor didn't last long. The minute Angus asked about how things were going, Ryan stiffened.

"Things are fine," he said shortly, knowing it didn't matter if things were good or bad. His parents had dumped him here because he'd been kicked out of private school—again—and they'd run out of places to send him. Angus's ranch was their last resort before sending him to a military academy. But Ryan was saving the pittance Angus paid him every month, and when he had enough money, he was leaving. He didn't know where he was going, he wasn't quite sure what he'd do when he got there. He only knew he wouldn't be contacting his parents ever again. They didn't want him. It seemed they'd never wanted him. And he was tired of everyone making him feel he was a burden. He wasn't a burden. He could take care of himself, and by God he would. "Things are just peachy."

"You don't sound like things are *peachy*."

Ryan glanced over at Angus. He had thinning red hair and probably would have freckles, too, except his skin was a leathery brown from spending so much time outside. At least fifty, he was in good physical condition, his shoulders broad, his arms well muscled, and he still had the energy of the younger guys who actually worked on the range. His pale blue eyes were calm, steady, and right now they were looking at Ryan in such a way that Ryan knew he wasn't going to get out of this conversation without giving an honest answer.

He sighed. If the old man wanted to play nice and try to make Ryan's life more bearable, Ryan decided to let him have a shot. After all, he hadn't blown a gasket over the drunk guy in the back.

"Geez, Angus," Ryan said, agitatedly combing his fingers through his thick yellow hair. "I'm the only hand who doesn't live in his own house or in the bunkhouse. I know you told my dad you'd take care of me, but that doesn't mean I have to live with you. Couldn't I at least live in the bunkhouse?"

For a few seconds Angus merely studied Ryan, obviously analyzing what Ryan had said. Ryan started to squirm. He hadn't realized how serious, how analytical the old coot was. In those few seconds Ryan saw that no one pulled the wool over this man's eyes—which was probably why Ryan's father had sent him here.

"I'm going to go out on a limb and bet that you don't really want to live in the bunkhouse as much as the guys are giving you a rough time about living with me."

Ryan slapped the steering wheel. "I'm getting prefer-

ential treatment," he said, angry now because all he really
wanted was to leave, to be on his own, to find people who
wanted him around. "The guys don't like it. I almost don't
blame them for taking it out on me."

"It's never appropriate to take out your frustration on
another person," Angus said, and Ryan got a tingly feeling
along the base of his spine, knowing Angus wasn't talking
about the ranch hands anymore, but about Ryan who was
obviously taking his frustration out on Angus now. The guy
was good. Ryan would give him that much.

The conversation took them to the dirt road that led to
Jackson Wright's house. Angus directed Ryan to turn the
Bronco, and they drove the next mile in total silence. At
first Ryan brooded over Angus having avoided his complaint with a tricky twist of conversation, but as they drove
farther down the road, Ryan began to squirm again. The
houses they passed were old and run-down—hell, most of
them were falling apart. Ryan knew this was his future once
he left Angus's Triple Moors Ranch, and though half of
him would gladly trade the lonely lap of luxury for self-
sufficiency and freedom, the other half knew there was
nothing fun about being cold and hungry.

Another house appeared in the distance and Angus
pointed. "That one."

"Okay," Ryan said quietly.

Ryan drove the Bronco down the long, thin dirt lane that
led to the dilapidated wood frame house. The day was hot
and dry. Heat seemed to make the world silent. Even the
Wrights' dog didn't move from the plank porch. Ryan
jerked the Bronco to a stop, and Angus jumped out.

Knowing Angus couldn't remove Jackson from the vehicle alone, Ryan assisted without hesitation. Together they
hauled Jackson up the porch steps and to the front door.

Though only a screen door separated the inside of the
Wright home from the rest of the world, Angus knocked

and waited. No one answered, but Ryan could hear the sound of a radio coming from the back of the house, probably the kitchen. Angus knocked again.

This time his knock was rewarded. Ryan heard the thump, thump, thump, of someone running down steps. Almost instantly a boy about Ryan's own age appeared on the other side of the screen door. About five foot six, reed thin and wearing cutoff jeans and a logo T-shirt, he looked like a typical teenager.

"Mr. MacFarland?" he said, confused. Then Ryan saw him notice his father. "Dad?"

"Your father's a little under the weather, son," Angus said kindly. "Show us the way to his room and we'll get him upstairs for you."

"Sure," the boy said, pushing the door back far enough that Ryan and Angus could drag Jackson through.

Although the place was small and the furniture worn, Ryan noticed that everything was neat as a pin. A young girl appeared from the back of the house, wiping her hands on a dish towel, and Ryan understood why the house, run-down as it was, really was a home. The girl was every bit as tall as her brother, but she appeared to be younger. Even from a distance Ryan could tell her eyes were pale blue, almost violet. Her hair was as dark as a stormcloud at midnight.

"What's wrong with Dad?" she asked anxiously.

"Your father is fine," Angus assured her, as he and Ryan guided Jackson up the first step of the stairs. "Perhaps the heat caused him to faint."

Angus didn't offer any more explanation, but the two kids didn't seem to require any. The young girl licked her lips as she watched Angus and Ryan maneuver her father up the short stairway. The boy couldn't quite meet Angus's eyes when he directed them into Jackson's bedroom. Nervous, he stayed in the hall, beyond the door, while Angus and Ryan laid Jackson on the bed.

"You two go on downstairs," Angus said to the boys, who silently watched as Angus loosened the top two buttons of Jackson's shirt. "I'll take care of business up here."

Jackson's son reluctantly turned away, but Ryan hovered by the bed. "Go on now, boy. Downstairs. I'll be along in a minute."

Ryan experienced a complicated series of emotions so strong he almost didn't know how to deal with them. He knew that Jackson was drunk, though Angus was too polite to say it. He was also astute enough to figure out that this meant trouble, not just for Jackson but for his two kids. This was a flagrant violation of ranch rules. Jackson hadn't merely endangered himself, he had endangered everyone who might have depended upon him today. Ryan knew, as well as both of Jackson's kids knew, that Angus would have no choice but to fire Jackson. And those two kids, poor as they already were, were about to get poorer.

Ryan was also observant and compassionate enough to understand Jackson's children didn't deserve this.

Unfortunately, Angus knew it, too. Ryan could see it in his eyes.

"Go on, boy. Downstairs."

Ryan left and Angus removed Jackson's boots then sat on the corner of the bed, feeling the weight of power press down on him. Firing somebody was never easy, but this time Angus had seen the faces of the innocent victims, and that made it worse. In a certain sense even Jackson himself wasn't at fault. He had a drinking problem and needed help. For years Angus had encouraged Jackson to seek treatment, but he never had, and now he'd crossed the line.

And Angus was faced with the consequences. Fire Jackson and ruin the lives of the two kids downstairs. Keep him and endanger the lives of his other hands.

"What're your names?"

Angus heard Ryan's voice drifting in through the open window and realized the kids had moved to the front porch.

"I'm Caleb...Cal," the young boy said. "And this is my sister, Grace."

"I'm Ryan Kelly. I work for Mr. MacFarland."

"You do?" Cal asked, sounding astounded. "You don't have to go to school?" Cal added that as if not having to go to school were the luckiest thing that could happen to a person.

"Well, yeah, if I'm still here in a few weeks, Angus will make me go to public school."

"I go to public school," Cal said, though not happily. "If you're still here, I'll show you around."

"Thanks, I'd appreciate that."

It was the first time since his arrival that Angus had heard Ryan talking normally to someone. He wasn't pretending to be tough for the hands. He wasn't raising hell, screaming and yelling about his rights as he threatened to run away. And he wasn't being overly respectful to Angus, knowing Angus held his fate in his hands. He was behaving normally. The sound was like music to Angus's ears.

"You're probably going to have to take chemistry this semester and I hear Mr. Dixon's a real pain in the butt. His tests are so hard, even smart kids fail."

"Great. Just great," Ryan muttered. "Now, on top of everything else, I guess I'll have to be studying, too."

Listening to the conversation and easy camaraderie being exchanged on the porch below, Angus sat up straighter. Suddenly a solution seemed obvious.

Ryan needed companionship. These two kids needed to have their father keep his job. If Angus were to put Jackson on the house staff, as a cook or a handyman, not only would Angus be able to keep an eye on Jackson, but Jackson wouldn't endanger anyone's life. Angus could also hire Cal and give him the same type of job Ryan had. A part-time, apprenticeship kind of position. Which would mean Ryan wouldn't be such an oddity on the ranch. He'd have a partner, an equal.

As a household employee Jackson would also get a block of rooms in the house—so Cal and Grace would live in the house—and Ryan wouldn't be the only hand living with Angus, which should be the end of the teasing about getting "preferential" treatment. It was perfect.

Angus patted Jackson's drunken rump as he walked by the bed. "I'll deal with you in the morning," he said, then smiled as he walked out of the room and closed the door.

Things were going to work out fine. Angus could feel it in his bones. Once he had a companion, Ryan would stay, lose his rebellious streak and do the right thing with his life. Angus didn't care if Ryan went his own way or decided to work in Graham Kelly's empire. He simply wanted to be sure that if Ryan chose a career other than following in his father's footsteps, he understood exactly what he was throwing away. As long as Angus had a few good years with the boy, he would ensure Ryan didn't make the wrong decision.

And maybe, just maybe, Angus thought, all of this might somehow compensate for his own failure as a father.

Chapter One

Sheriff Ryan Kelly waited in the shadows behind a cement pillar of a parking garage. His charge, Madison Delaney, a witness for a burglary trial, refused protection, but her best friend, District Attorney Jessica Whitaker, assigned Ryan and his deputy to keep an eye on her anyway.

After two weeks of inconspicuously making sure her path was clear, hovering in corners outside her meeting rooms and watching her house until his deputy relieved him, Ryan was tired and bored. But he still agreed with Jessica. In spite of the fact that nothing had happened thus far, the very public Delaney should be taking this situation more seriously.

Ryan sighed and nestled his back against the cool column. He knew, of course, that she wouldn't. Having grown up the son of a bank president turned entrepreneur, Ryan knew all about people like Madison Delaney. As owner of Kidtastic, a company that made anything and everything for children, she worked her tail off by day, then socialized with the right people at night. In an odd kind of way Madison Delaney was actually a combination of both his parents, the breadwinner and the master socializer all rolled into one, which, he now realized, was probably why she refused protection. An escort would hamper her ability to run her normal schedule.

Shaking his head, Ryan knew he would never understand why some people felt the world revolved around money. He was glad he only had to guard Madison Delaney, not live with her, not even get to know her.

As he had that last thought, the elevator doors opened and tall, blond, beautiful Madison emerged. Her medium-length hair softly framed her face, and her peach suit accented every curve of her body, showcasing her long, long legs. Like always, Ryan's mouth watered, but he stopped it easily because he knew who and what she was. He could protect her—he could protect anybody—that was his job. But there was no way in hell he wanted to get involved with her because there was no way anyone could get him to approve of a lifestyle he knew was dead wrong.

Careful to keep himself hidden behind the concrete pillar, Ryan began to stand, but before he'd completely risen, shots rang out from the far corner of the garage.

As Madison Delaney stepped off her private elevator into the basement parking garage of her building, something whizzed by her ear. The sound it made was loud and different. Not like anything she'd ever heard before. She had time to register that the noise couldn't have been an insect, then she heard a pop, then the whiz again, and knew the objects flying by her ear were bullets. Someone was shooting at her.

Someone was shooting at her!

The very second she made the connection, strong arms grabbed her from behind. Terrified, she kicked and squealed, but her attacker put his hand over her mouth and mumbled, "For God's sake, Ms. Delaney, don't fight me! I'm Sheriff Ryan Kelly. I'll be happy to show you ID as soon as I get you out of this mess."

The next thing Madison knew, she was thrown behind a thick concrete column. Shielding her body with his own, her attacker turned into her rescuer and pointed his gun in the direction of the shots being fired. He got off two rounds before tires squealed in the far corner of the garage and the scent of exhaust fumes filled the air. Two more shots erupted. Sheriff Kelly also fired two more times. Then as quickly as the whole episode began, it was over. With a roar, the car containing the gunmen flew up the short ramp, through the open entryway and into the night.

Frightened out of her wits, Madison slapped Sheriff Kelly's shoulder with her clutch bag. "What the hell is going on here?"

"As far as I could tell, I just saved your life," he said, then grabbed her hands and hauled her to her feet. A shock of straight sandy brown hair had fallen to his forehead in his struggle to save her, but otherwise he was perfectly composed. His hands were steady and strong. His unwavering blue eyes searched hers. "You okay?"

Scared, numb, but basically unhurt, Madison nodded. Sheriff Kelly wasn't wearing a uniform, but he had on a pair of loose-fitting jeans and an old gray sweatshirt, both of which highlighted his trim, well-muscled body. From the lack of lines on his face, Madison guessed his age to be about thirty...and he'd saved her. If he hadn't been hiding in the shadows, she would have been killed. *Killed!* Shot in her own damned parking garage.

"Come on, then, let's get the hell out of here in case those guys change their minds and decide to come back and finish the job."

"But why would anyone shoot at me?" she asked,

scrambling beside Ryan as he dragged her toward a police car, which had been hidden in the dark corner behind them.

"Who would want to shoot at me?" he mocked, then he shoved her into the passenger seat of his car. He slammed the door and jogged around the car's hood. He wasted no time getting into the driver's side, behind the wheel, then he reached into his back pocket and pulled out his wallet. As he showed her his ID, he said, "You're testifying against a gang of thieves who have eluded capture for ten years. They'll do anything to keep you from reaching the witness stand." He snapped his wallet closed. "It's a good thing your friend, the DA, decided to ignore your refusal of police protection."

As Sheriff Kelly drove his car out of the parking garage and into the street, Madison sighed and fell back against the seat. Her thick yellow hair created a sort of pillow for her, cushioning her head. But her heart still pounded furiously in her chest, her legs felt like gelatin. She hadn't forgotten that she was testifying against a gang of crooks. She also hadn't thought these criminals were harmless. She thought she was safe since the burglars were denied bail.

Confused, she glanced at Ryan Kelly. "Those crooks are in jail. How could they possibly try to kill me?"

"Even criminals have friends, lady."

Up to now, she could give the sheriff the benefit of the doubt and think he was as jumpy as she was after having been shot at and that's why everything he said sounded rude. But that last remark, well, that was nothing but an insult.

"Sheriff Kelly, save your attitude for somebody else. I don't want to hear it. I also don't want you calling me 'lady.' I find it insulting. My name is Madison or Ms. Delaney. And that's what you can call me."

"I know your name." He paused, sighed. "*Everybody* knows your name." He took his eyes off the road to glare at her. "All the more reason why you desperately needed someone to guard you."

And all the more reason not to want a bunch of policemen invading her privacy, discovering her secrets, Madison thought, though she didn't say anything—wouldn't say anything—until she was absolutely positive Ryan Kelly could be trusted.

She faced him again. "Where are we going?"

"To my uncle's ranch. It's fairly far out of town. You'll be safe there."

"Will I get to use a phone soon?"

"When we get to the ranch. And don't ask to use the cellular," Ryan said, laying his hand on the case as if to secure it. "These transmissions are too easily monitored."

"I know that," she snapped, angry now because things had gotten so far out of control that a sanctimonious policeman was threatening her as if she didn't have a brain in her head.

She stopped her thoughts. *Things* had not gotten out of control. One part of her life had gotten out of control. The important part, her daughter Lacy, was very well protected. Which served to reenforce her decision to keep her daughter hidden from the press and public. If anyone knew about her daughter, Lacy would be the crooks' target, not Madison herself.

Calmer about little Lacy but still irritated with the sanctimonious policeman beside her, she settled herself against the car seat. "Even if I were calling my mother, I'm smart enough to prefer something a little more private."

Ryan drew in a long breath. "Sorry," he said, and Madison could tell he meant it. His deep, smooth voice, a voice that could easily sooth a cranky child, or woo a lover, filled the car with sincerity.

She felt small and foolish, not merely for snapping at him, but also for doubting her system. That system was too good—too damned good—to fail. The only failure here would be caused by Madison's impatience.

After thirty minutes of absolute silence, Ryan pulled the car into the long, tree-lined lane of a ranch, and Madison began to relax, knowing they were reaching their destination and that soon she'd have a chance to talk with Jessica. She wanted Jessica's word, not Ryan Kelly's, about what happened next.

The minute they stepped into the wooden foyer of the rustic two-story main house of the ranch, she turned to Ryan. "I need to make a phone call."

"*I* need to make a phone call first," he said.

"But mine's—"

"I'm calling Jessica," he said, cutting her off. "To let her know you're safe and to get instructions."

"Actually, I was calling Jessica, too."

"Then you can talk with her after I'm done."

The words weren't fully out of Ryan's mouth, when a raven-haired woman came bounding down the steps. "Hi," she greeted cheerfully.

"Here. That's my sister, Grace," he said, turning Madison in the direction of the two-tiered steps which were padded in the center with pale green carpet. The light-colored strip and the scattered pictures on the walls gave the only relief from the polished wooden floors and walls of the unpretentious foyer. "Grace, this is Madison Delaney."

"*The* Madison Delaney?"

"*The* Madison Delaney," Ryan agreed, gently shoving Madison toward the woman jogging down the steps. "Get her a drink. I just saved her from an ambush."

"Really?" Grace asked. Her violet eyes grew big with curiosity. Her full mouth bowed upward into a delighted smile.

"Don't ask questions, Grace. Take her into the living room and get her some brandy. I'll be right out."

With those words he was gone, and Grace turned and smiled at Madison. "He's not actually my brother. Angus sort of raised us both. I got the class. He got the courage. Come on, I'll get you that drink."

Since she knew she'd be talking with Jessica in a few minutes, Madison didn't argue. She followed Grace into a small, cluttered living room. White brocade furniture was littered with sections of the newspaper. An open book lay facedown on an end table. Computer printouts decorated sections of the hardwood floor and the wine-colored print accent rug.

"Don't pay any attention to this mess," Grace said as she began to gather the paper. "I had to move out when I decided to get my MBA. Since then the house has gone to hell."

"Don't worry about it," Madison said, finding the jumble strangely endearing. The place wasn't really dirty, it merely looked lived in. After being shot at, sitting in a lived-in home was surprisingly comforting.

Still gathering old newspapers, Grace said, "I've tried bringing someone in to straighten up, but every time I retain new help, the boys scare them off. I've even tried hiring a male housekeeper, somebody big and strapping who could yell right back at them, but nobody ever lasts."

"That's because we all like a house that's comfortable."

Madison turned at the sound of the soft male voice and saw a tall, balding man standing in the entryway. Though shaded with streaks of white, Madison could tell that the hair he had left had once been bright red.

"This is Angus," Grace said. "Father figure."

"Father figure, hell," Angus said, accepting Grace's hug. "I *am* your father. I adopted you." He paused long enough to look at Madison. "Who is this?"

"Madison Delaney. Ryan rescued her from an ambush."

"Who would ambush a helpless woman?"

"Angus, women aren't called helpless anymore," Grace chastened in a whisper.

"That's okay, Grace," Madison said, settling herself on the sofa when Angus offered it with a motion of his hand. "I was being shot at because I'm the primary witness in a case against some burglars."

"Oh, you're the gal who caught the thieves from Overland Township."

Not in the mood for small-talk, Madison peeked at her watch. She had a good twenty minutes before anyone would miss her, and logic told her everything was okay. She'd taken too many precautions. Because her syndicated column ran in all the major papers, her name, like Erma Bombeck's, had become a household word. Since she was a single woman writing about raising children, tabloid speculation ran toward guessing when she'd marry and have her own child. When Madison became pregnant and didn't marry Lacy's father, she knew the tabloids would go wild trying to discover Lacy's dad's identity and to uncover the story of why Madison refused to marry him. So, to save herself that misery, she told her staff she was on vacation in Hawaii, and spent her final pregnancy months living in the Colorado mountains, conducting business via conference call, fax and modem.

But after she had Lacy, she not only recognized that the story would be even juicier now that she was no longer pregnant but actually had an adorable baby, she also saw that keeping Lacy a secret had some other pluses, as well. First, because Lacy had such a famous mother, there was no way she could have a normal childhood, so she needed a little "insulation" from the world. Second, ultimately it would be Lacy not Madison who would suffer because Lacy "didn't have" a dad. Third, keeping Lacy hidden protected her from all the crooks and cranks, and just plain nuts, who frequently clung to celebrities.

Because of all this, a mere handful of people knew Madison had a daughter, and that handful of people was well trained to protect Madison's little girl. Lacy's entourage was the only reason Jessica let Madison get away with no bodyguards. Lacy had more protection than an armored car. Still, getting shot at left Madison shaken enough to doubt her nearly flawless system, and she knew she'd feel much better once she talked with Jessica.

Hiding her anxiety, she smiled at Angus and Grace. "I didn't catch the robbers, I simply got unlucky and overheard them planning their next job."

"You were wise to turn them in."

"I didn't think I had a choice," Madison answered honestly, then took the brandy Grace handed her. "I normally don't drink," she began, but Angus silenced her with a wave of his hand.

"You had a scare. If Ryan said you need brandy, you need brandy."

"Ryan sort of bosses everybody around," Grace supplied when Madison threw Angus a questioning look. "He's the oldest, so he thinks he runs the place."

From the high-handed way he'd treated her, Madison could certainly relate to that. Glancing at the painting above the mantel of the stone fireplace, Madison saw Ryan, Grace and another young man clustered around Angus. "Then Ryan is your real son?" she asked, knowing that Grace was adopted.

"Heavens, no," Angus said with a laugh. "Belongs to friends of mine, Graham and Althea Kelly. He didn't like going to boarding school and ended up here at the ranch. Been in Crossroads Creek ever since."

Madison glanced at her watch again.

"Something wrong?" Angus asked, his Scottish accent

finding its way into his words in spite of his attempts to stop it.

Calling upon poise gained from years of practice, Madison shook her head and smiled. "No, I'm fine." Hoping to distract her host, she pointed at the picture. "You certainly make a lovely family."

Peering at her, Angus said, "That's because we worked at it. I decided we needed to be a family, so that's what we became. That also means I'm perceptive, that I know when I'm getting the runaround. I can see something's troubling you, girl. Might as well be out with it."

"You might as well," Grace said from beside Madison. "He'll hound you until you confess every sin on your soul. Come clean now, and save yourself the interrogation."

Madison swallowed.

Ryan listened to the sound of Jessica's office phone ringing once, twice, three times, and he started sweating, thinking she'd already gone for the day and that he would waste the next hour or two tracking her down. Luckily she picked it up on the fourth ring. "Where the hell were you?"

"Finishing a meeting," Jessica answered pleasantly "Why?"

"I've got Madison Delaney, that's why."

From the quick indrawn breath, Ryan knew Jessica understood what he was telling her. "What happened?" she asked without preamble.

"Someone shot at her in the parking garage. I grabbed her in the nick of time."

"Good Lord. Thank God we had the foresight to protect her."

"Yeah, we're terrifically smart," Ryan said. "So, what do we do with her now that she understands she needs protection?"

"I don't know," Jessica answered, and Ryan could

imagine her combing her fingers through her dark brown hair and taking a seat behind her cluttered desk.

"This *is* a problem," she mumbled, as if working out the full implications of the situation in her head. "Oh, boy, is this a problem. She can't go back home," Jessica continued, thinking aloud. "She can't come to my house, it's too obvious."

Ryan thought of the five-foot-nine hellcat he'd pulled out of the path of several bullets. He remembered how she'd slapped his shoulder with her purse and yelled at him just because he'd called her lady. He also remembered the fire in her amber-colored eyes, the way her thick yellow hair bobbed when she angrily tossed her head and the fact that as owner of an entire company this was a woman who wasn't accustomed to taking orders from anybody. Knowing he was probably going to regret this, Ryan rubbed his hand across the back of his neck. "I sort of have a plan," he said, grimacing.

"I'm all ears."

"Angus has a cabin up in the mountains. He uses it for fishing. It's a good hour's drive away."

"I know where it is. Angus had a picnic up there two years ago, remember?"

"Yeah, that's right. Which means you know it's very private, and we could hide your friend there indefinitely if we had to."

"Actually, it's exactly what we need, Ryan."

"And no one followed us here, so if we get ourselves moving right now, I could have her at the cabin before anybody even realized she was missing."

"Great. Wonderful. This is perfect. Getting her out of town is probably the best thing we can do."

"That's what I thought," Ryan agreed.

"And no one, but no one, should know where she is. Because we still don't know who these guys were working for, we don't know who we're dealing with and who can get to her or how. In fact, I don't think I'll tell anybody here in my office where we've taken her or even that we have her," Jessica added, obviously planning as she spoke.

"Don't even tell her staff."

Jessica paused and finally said, "I have to tell them something."

"Then tell them she's on vacation."

When she didn't answer, Ryan knew Jessica was considering that. "They'll probably figure out that the trial has something to do with this sudden vacation, but that won't matter as long they don't know where she is."

"Exactly," Ryan said.

"Okay, go get her. I'll break the bad news to her that she's leaving town without packing."

"Fine by me," Ryan said.

"Uh, Ryan," Jessica continued, "I don't want you in the room with her when I explain to her what we've got to do. Give her some privacy. Wait outside the door for her."

A little confused, but not concerned, because he trusted Jessica's judgment implicitly, Ryan said, "Sure. Fine. Whatever."

He set the receiver beside the phone and started up the hall to the living room. Outside the door he heard Angus's low voice. "I seriously didn't mind that Rachel had a child without a husband," he said solemnly. "What troubled me was that she seemed to be very unconcerned about the effect of her problems on her child."

Peering around the door frame, Ryan could see both Madison and Grace staring at Angus with rapt attention. Leaning forward, palming her brandy glass, Madison said, "Had someone said something or done something to make you feel this way?"

Angus shook his head. "Truthfully, no," he admitted.

"But twenty-five years ago, times were different. People weren't as accepting as they are now."

"No, you're right," Madison agreed.

"But I really wasn't right," Angus said. "Rachel and I argued all the time. I said a lot of things I didn't mean. And then one day we had a major argument. Rachel had come home after a two-week trip away to 'find' herself. She said she now knew what she wanted to do…start her own business. I was tired and concerned for Rachel's daughter—my *granddaughter*—Alexis because she'd been without her mother for so long. Yet Rachel didn't seem all that worried about it. Anyway, I asked her when she was going to get a daddy for Alex, and Rachel exploded. She called me judgmental and cruel. I called her irresponsible and doubly cruel for leaving her seven-month-old daughter alone on a ranch for weeks at a time. Rachel told me to take it back, but I refused. I told her to grow up. She told me to go to hell. I told her to leave…and not to come back." He stopped, licked his dry lips. "She hasn't."

"Why didn't you ever try to find her?"

Angus glanced at her sharply. "I did find her. She owns an advertising agency in New York City. She's successful, wealthy, healthy and wise. She's doing very well. She doesn't need me." He paused, studied his hands, then looked at Madison again. "And I don't beg."

Stunned, Ryan stood in the doorway staring at Angus. Never, ever had he told that story to anyone. Ryan only knew it because his parents knew it. He didn't have a clue what Madison had said to get Angus to open up to her, but whatever it was it must have been good. And whatever it was, Ryan didn't want her saying it again. Once was enough to hear Angus go through the anguish of reliving that moment of his life.

He strode into the room. "Jessica wants to talk with

you," he said, probably a little more angrily than he'd intended, because he felt defensive for Angus.

"Thank you," Madison said, rising from the sofa.

"The phone's this way," Ryan directed gruffly, but he paused, glancing at Angus who sat watching the spot on the floor above his shoes.

"Don't just stand there," Angus said, when he realized Ryan was looking at him rather than doing his duty, "get her to the phone. She's got business to take care of."

Chapter Two

Ryan led Madison to the den. Without a word he pointed to the phone, then walked out of the room. When the closed door separated him from his five-foot-nine "baby-sitting assignment," he pinched the bridge of his nose and squeezed his eyes shut. The next two weeks would be the longest of his life.

Resigned, he started up the hall to the living room again to inform Angus he was borrowing his fishing cabin.

"Of course you can use the cabin," Angus said, his voice booming from behind the bar. "Why is it we never have any Scotch in this house anymore?"

"Because you're not allowed to drink it," Ryan said, settling himself on the chair across from the sofa.

"That's never stopped him before."

Ryan glanced at Cal who had joined Angus and Grace in the living room while Ryan had taken Madison Delaney to the phone. In the same way that Ryan thought of Grace as his sister, he also thought of Cal as a brother. Almost the same age, Cal and Ryan shared enough physical qualities that they could have passed for bothers. Both were tall and thin. Both had sandy brown hair.

"That would be why we're hiding it from him," Ryan said, giving Cal a pointed look.

"You're hiding it from me," Angus said as he jumped up from behind the bar.

"The doctor said your blood pressure's too high," Grace said, patting the sofa cushion next to her, hinting that Angus should move away from the bar and sit beside her. "Get your blood pressure down and you'll get your Scotch back."

"There's a comfort," Angus said and joined her on the couch.

"So," Cal said, obviously changing the subject. "I hear I missed all the excitement."

"No, the excitement is still in the den, holding a *personal* conversation with the DA."

Cal grinned at Ryan. "Sounds like somebody's jealous."

"Of the DA?" Ryan scoffed. "Not hardly."

"The DA is a woman…*Jessica* Whitaker," Grace reminded Cal. "But that doesn't necessarily mean Ryan isn't jealous."

"Of what?"

"Oh, come on, lad," Angus cajoled, his blue eyes shining. "I noticed your cheeks growing red when you came into the room to call Miss Delaney to the phone."

"Probably because I'm angry with her."

"That's a new twist on an old theme," Cal said, laughing.

"I *am* angry," Ryan said, then rose and started to pace. "Not only do I have to give up the next two weeks of my life to baby-sit a woman I know isn't going to listen to a damned word I say—"

"Two weeks?" Grace asked, interrupting Ryan.

"The trial doesn't start for another two weeks."

"You're spending two weeks, alone, in a cabin in the woods with a woman even Angus describes as 'quite a looker,'" Cal said, then he whistled. "Lord, you're in deep trouble."

"I am not in deep trouble," Ryan insisted. "But Madison is and she doesn't seem—"

"Ah, first names already," Angus said, smirking. "There's a good sign."

"Will you give it a rest?" Ryan said.

Just then Madison Delaney sheepishly appeared in the living room entryway. She wasn't nervous the way she had been on the drive up. Discovering she would be safe for the next two weeks obviously took a major burden from her mind. But beyond that Ryan also noticed her full pink lips were bowed upward in a smile and her light brown eyes shone devilishly as if she'd heard ample conversation to know Ryan's family had been teasing him.

While taking his shifts of guarding her, Ryan saw firsthand that Madison Delaney got public relations and advertising advantages a normal business person wouldn't because she was one sexy entrepreneur. For the past two weeks he'd ignored her bouncy blond hair, her nearly perfect figure and her long, long legs, because he had a job to do. But seeing her now, there was a part of him that was wickedly tempted to do exactly as his family expected and let the chips fall where they may in the next two weeks. He felt his face turn red as a beet again and cursed his fair skin.

Angus, Cal and Grace burst into laughter.

"Let's go," Ryan said, grabbing his Stetson from the coffee table. "I promised Jessica I'd have you at the cabin before anybody has time to miss you."

He started for the door, but Madison stopped him. "That's all you're taking?" she ventured uncertainly.

"We'll get food along the way."

"Well, I was hoping for a change of clothes. Don't I even get to stop at my house for jeans and a sweater?"

"Are you kidding?" Ryan said with a gasp. "That's the last place you can go right now."

"I have to spend the next two weeks wearing this?" Madison asked, glancing down at her wrinkled peach suit. The skirt had two dirt smudges, probably from their scuffle in the parking garage.

Grace sprang from the sofa. "Come upstairs with me. I keep lots of jeans, T-shirts and sweatsuits here. You can borrow anything you like."

"Thanks," Madison said, then followed Grace from the room.

When Ryan faced Cal and Angus, both were gaping at him. "Are you planning on staying in the same clothes for the next two weeks?" Angus asked incredulously. "Or does she have you so smitten, you're already not thinking straight?"

"Neither," Ryan said. "I have plenty of things up at the cabin."

"Yeah, nice, smelly old fishing clothes," Cal said, picking up the newspaper as if the conversation didn't interest him. "That ought to go a long way toward convincing your witness that you're trustworthy."

Despite the fact that there was little logic to what Cal said, Ryan sighed heavily, turned on his heel and went to his bedroom to shove some things into a duffel bag.

Twenty minutes later they were in the car. Not only had Grace provided comfortable clothes for Madison, but she'd convinced Madison to change into jeans and a T-shirt for the long drive to the mountains. While all this was happening, Angus rousted his cook to throw some groceries into a box, and Cal checked under the hood of Ryan's Bronco.

"Your family certainly is interesting," Madison said,

smiling to herself at the memory of the entire MacFarland clan banding together not merely to see to her safety, but also to see to her comfort. Unfortunately she felt a surge of guilt, as well, because so many people were taking care of business for her. Not merely the MacFarlands, but Jessica also.

Rather than take any chances, Jessica had agreed to bring Lacy to the cabin. But Madison drew the line at forcing Jessica to be the one to tell Sheriff Kelly that he had another party to guard. Though bossy Mr. Thinks-He's-Perfect Ryan Kelly was the last person Madison wanted to confide in about her baby, she had no choice but to tell him the truth, the whole truth and nothing but the truth...and that wasn't going to be easy.

"Yeah, they're interesting all right," Ryan said, but Madison noticed he wouldn't look at her.

"You're not angry with them for teasing you, are you?"

"No, though I should be." He spared her a quick, emotionless glance. "How much of that conversation did you hear, anyway?"

"Only enough to know that your family has an excellent sense of humor."

"Which means you heard just about everything."

"My conversation with Jessica wasn't very long."

"That's peachy."

"So I heard from the point where Angus was complaining about Scotch."

"You heard it all then."

A long silence settled over them, and though Madison knew what she had to say, she simply couldn't find the courage to say it. This man with the wonderful family had the sense of humor of a rock, and he wasn't going to take the news lightly that her seven-month-old daughter would be joining them. From the way he behaved, Ryan Kelly hadn't made a mistake in his life. If he had, he wouldn't admit it. He also didn't seem to like her very much. Plus, he didn't like complications and details. Lacy was both.

After a few minutes of no sound but the whine of tires rolling across the pavement, Ryan cautiously said, "I don't understand why you refused protection."

Though his comment was weighted with criticism, Madison felt Ryan had unexpectedly given her her chance to explain about Lacy by explaining why she refused protection.

"You don't have to answer if you don't want to," Ryan said, when she didn't respond right away.

"Actually, Mr. Kelly, the reason I refused protection is a secret."

He glanced at her, saw she was serious, and his mouth fell open. "You're joking, right?"

"Well, maybe I phrased that wrong. My reason for refusing protection isn't a secret itself. My reason for refusing protection is because of a secret."

"Oh, that makes sense."

"It does because—" she began, ready to break into an explanation about Lacy, but Ryan Kelly interrupted her.

"Well, I don't buy it," he angrily retorted. "I think you were just being plain stubborn."

Madison gaped at him. "You can't honestly believe I'd refuse protection simply because I'm stubborn."

"It's been known to happen."

"Not to me. I'm too much of a business person to be that foolish. As with any other decision, I weighed the pros and cons and decided it was worth the risk to assume that the crooks couldn't hurt me, since they were in prison. I also took some extra precautions to protect…myself… because I didn't want a bunch of policemen snooping around my house."

"Because of your secret?"

She nodded, relieved that he seemed to be understanding. "Because of my secret."

"That's bull."

Amazed that he could be so self-righteous, particularly when he didn't have all the facts yet, she stared at him. "Don't you have any secrets, Mr. Kelly?"

"My life's an open book."

"Oh, really? Then explain why you live with Angus MacFarland, a woman who's not your sister and a man who's not your brother. You can't tell me there's not a secret in that."

"There isn't. I was raised by Angus because my parents more or less abandoned me," Ryan said casually, as if this kind of information were given out every day.

"Your parents abandoned you?" Madison asked incredulously, sympathetic in spite of herself.

Ryan laughed, but without much real humor. "My parents weren't derelicts, Ms. Delaney, simply workaholics, and busy people don't have time for children."

"That's ridiculous," Madison said, her spine stiffening. "Not all people who are busy have *abandoned* their children."

"You think?" Ryan asked, sparing her a glance again. "You can believe what you want to believe, but I can tell you from experience that being ignored is exactly like being abandoned. The way it seemed to me, my parents thought the world should be made up of adults, because adults can care for themselves. When they realized I couldn't take care of myself, they hid me."

"Hid you?" Madison choked.

"Well, they didn't exactly put me in a closet with bread and water. They simply hired nannies and baby-sitters to keep me busy and occupied while they went to dinners and charity balls and entertained for themselves."

Not knowing how to respond, Madison merely stared at

him. In spite of the fact that the circumstances were totally different, he could have been describing how she raised Lacy.

"When I got old enough, I was shuffled from one world-class boarding school to another. I'd come home for holidays and vacations, but my parents had commitments and basically spent very little time with me. When they did have a moment to spare, they'd use it to tell me how wonderful it would be when I took over the family business. But I didn't want the family business. As far as I was concerned that's what kept my parents away from me, and I wouldn't ever do anything that would keep me away from my kids—when I had them.

"One day I got fed up and I ran away. But they found me. So, I ran away again. And they found me again. That went on at least six times, until Angus intervened and offered to take me off my parents' hands."

He paused, glanced at Madison, his blue eyes seeking her gaze in the darkened car. "They accepted his offer and here I am. I see them some holidays and *occasionally* spend a week of summer vacation with them at one of their villas, but otherwise I'm in Crossroads Creek. And I've never been happier." He paused again, sought her gaze again. "And before you ask, neither have they. Dad has his companies and Mother has her charities. They're busy and happy. This situation suits all of us."

Stunned, Madison had absolutely no idea of what to say. The things Madison did to hide Lacy were designed to shield her from the press and the public. But given what he'd just said, Madison didn't think Ryan would see it that way.

"I'm sure your parents had their reasons."

"They did have their reasons for leaving me alone," he reported casually. "They didn't have time for a child in their lives." He snagged her gaze again. "Really, Ms. Delaney, it's that simple."

Madison swallowed. "Sometimes things aren't always as they seem."

"There were no 'secrets' in my parents' lives. They didn't need any more money. There was no big family debt to pay, and no family legacy to hold on to. Personally, I think they liked the glamour of being important, though I can't see what the attraction is. Why anyone would go to such great lengths to stay in the public eye is beyond me." As if finally realizing he was describing her lifestyle, Ryan stopped and glanced at her. He sucked in a long draft of air, then expelled it on a deep sigh. "Sorry."

All of Madison's muscles tightened. The blood that flowed through her veins was so cool and so slow she could have frozen him with one concentrated stare. "I don't like the glamour of being important. Being important didn't motivate me to start companies or to write my syndicated column. Providing jobs for my employees did. Paying the bills, caring for my parents, giving my brothers and sisters a start in life, all those things got and keep me going."

"I said I was sorry."

"Just like you grew up feeling abandoned by your parents," she continued angrily, not merely because she was insulted by what he'd said, but also because he was wrong. Not everything was as simple, as cut and dry, as it must have seemed to him as a boy. At least it wasn't for her. If she didn't spend as much time as she did keeping her companies prosperous, Lacy wouldn't merely grow up fatherless, she'd grow up poor.

And that was the one thing Madison couldn't tolerate.

"I grew up feeling worthless because my family was poor. Working—being needed—gives me a sense of self-worth. Working also gives my life meaning and purpose. But beyond all that, I have a gift. I use it. Because I use it, many, many people have jobs. Good jobs. I'm not ashamed of that.''

Madison stopped herself and drew in a long breath. In all of Lacy's life she'd never had to defend her decision on how to raise her daughter, and of all the angles of that decision to have to defend, working hard to provide a good life for her child would have been the last she would have suspected someone would criticize.

Still, arguing with Ryan Kelly about this was irrelevant and foolish. Whether she wanted to or not, she *had* to tell him about Lacy. But this was absolutely, positively the wrong time to do it. If she told him about Lacy now, he'd jump to the conclusion that she was exactly like his parents, and the next two weeks would be a living, breathing, fiery hell. There was no way she'd accept a constant stream of criticism for two weeks, and no way this guy could hold his sanctimonious tongue.

She sighed and glanced at her watch. With all the bundling and packing Jessica would have to do to get Lacy ready for the trip, she would be at least an hour behind them. There was plenty of time to let this particular discussion die a natural death before she tried to explain in the nicest way possible that she had a child and she didn't care to hear his opinion of that.

She looked out the window. If ever two people were complete opposites and not meant to spend any time at all together, they were the inhabitants of this car.

It was going to be a long two weeks.

Ryan stared at the road in front of him. Part of him realized he'd opened his mouth a little too wide and if he hadn't stopped when he had, his size-twelve sneakers would be about choking him now. The other part of him thought it didn't matter, since he had a right to his opinions. Not only had his childhood been hell, but if Miss Madison Delaney didn't get her head out of her secretive clouds and follow his instructions to the letter over the next two weeks her life would be in danger. That was simple, straightforward reality. But she didn't want to be reminded of reality. She believed in secrets, while he believed in facts.

If ever two people were complete opposites and not meant to spend long periods of time alone, they were the two people headed for the solitude of Angus's cabin.

He sighed. It was going to be a long two weeks.

Chapter Three

When they pulled up beside the cabin, Madison opened her door and jumped out. She drew her duffel bag full of Grace's clothes from the back seat, then followed Ryan as he strode to the porch. The sky was filled with dark clouds, and the cabin itself was surrounded by trees, and Madison couldn't see much walking up the stone path. But it didn't matter. She'd have two whole weeks to look around.

"There's a generator in the outbuilding at the end of the lane," Ryan said, pushing open the front door with his shoulder as he pocketed his key. Once inside, he grabbed one of the two flashlights which sat on the shelf by the front door. "After I take a quick look around in here I need to go over and start up the generator before we'll have lights, but you can wait inside for me if you don't mind sitting alone in the dark."

"I'll be fine," she said quietly, deciding a few more minutes couldn't hurt. If it had taken her and Ryan over an hour to drive to this cabin, it would take Jessica longer. A change of scenery and a few minutes of privacy were exactly what they needed to distance themselves from their last conversation. Then she would tell him about Lacy.

"Okay. I'll go get the generator now," Ryan said, returning from his quick inspection of the cabin to make sure they were alone. He handed her the other flashlight. "You can use this to find your way around while I'm gone."

"Thanks," Madison said. She flipped the switch that turned on the flashlight and strolled the beam in a circle around the huge room. Furnished with comfortable overstuffed floral furniture and sporting a stone fireplace and round braided rugs on hardwood floors the "cabin" wasn't anything like Madison expected. Impressed, she cautiously edged her way into the room.

Pictures of Grace, Cal and Ryan in various stages of growing up sat on the end tables and the mantel. After dropping her duffel bag to the floor in front of the cold hearth, Madison lifted one of the pictures.

"This is Angus's home away from home. He comes up here when he wants to be alone to think. He usually doesn't let us come with him. That's why he's got pictures everywhere."

Surprised, Madison spun around. Ryan stood in the darkness, haloed in the yellow glow from his flashlight. The pale illumination shadowed his features, making him appear dark and mysterious, dangerous and sexy. For a good thirty seconds she stood spellbound, staring at him, for the first time realizing that she would be alone with him...alone with a very appealing man in a cabin so far away from the rest of the world that even the bears only used this area as a vacation spot.

Little prickles of awareness rose on her forearms. Her breath quivered. It had been years, literally years, since a man had tempted her beyond reason, but she still recognized the symptoms. Regardless of over two hours of antagonism, she found Ryan Kelly irresistibly attractive—at least physically. In some ways that scared her more than knowing her burglars might still be looking for her.

Ryan flicked a switch and bathed the room in bright yellow light, revealing the dust and cobwebs that the darkness had neatly hidden, and turning himself back into the cynical policeman who'd saved her a few hours before. She almost breathed a sigh of relief.

"It's a beautiful cabin."

"It's a dirty cabin," Ryan disagreed, hoisting his duffel bag to a convenient chair and turning toward the door again. "I'll get the groceries."

When he was gone, Madison did breathe a sigh of relief. She blamed her reaction to him on being overtired, then decided she'd better tell Ryan about Lacy while she still had some of her wits about her.

When Ryan returned, she smiled brightly and was just about to open her mouth to speak, but he didn't stop in the living room. Carrying a box of supplies, he veered to the right and walked through a door which she presumed led to the kitchen. Madison heard the sound of the box hitting a hard surface, then he reappeared at the door. "There are two more bags of groceries," he said. "I'll need another minute. Are you sure you're okay?"

"I'm fine," Madison said, but she glanced at her watch. Time was running out on her.

Seeing her dismay, Ryan peered into her face, as if looking at her for the first time, and Madison felt odd prickles of fire dance down her spine. At that point she absolutely knew she was too, too tired to be alone with him. He was rude, he was cynical, he was abrupt and bossy. Yet she was breathtakingly attracted to him.

"You're sure?"

She nodded. "Positive."

"Okay," Ryan said, pointing toward a black metal spiral staircase. "There are three bedrooms. Two upstairs and one down here. I thought we should both take a room upstairs. In case anything happens, I won't be too far away. If you'd like I could show you up now and you could start to unpack while I get the rest of the supplies.''

She wasn't really sure she had time to completely unpack before she told him about Lacy, but the little distraction of taking her things to a room and puttering around for a minute might be exactly what she needed to give her back her sanity.

''That's a good idea,'' Madison said and allowed him to lead her up the stairs to the bedroom at the end of the hall. The room was furnished with a light pine bed and dressers. A no-nonsense red-and-blue-plaid spread covered the bed. Curtains in the same print hung on the windows. She dumped her duffel on the bed.

''Bathroom's down the hall,'' Ryan informed casually, pointing to the right, and Madison felt her mouth go dry. The tiny room made him seem big and tall. His worn Stetson and denim jacket made him rugged and masculine. In this small room, even his bossy, domineering personality didn't come across as being offensive. Instead he seemed powerful, masterful. Sensual in that way only real, honest-to-God rugged men could be. Her heart trembled in her chest. The temperature suddenly seemed way too warm.

''But there won't be any hot water for at least an hour, so you won't be able to shower or bathe.''

''That's fine,'' Madison said, nearly pushing him out of the room. When he left, she fell to the foot of the bed and dropped her head to her hands, praying the strange reactions she felt around Ryan Kelly were simply the result of being tired. The last thing in the world she needed was to be attracted to him, but more than that she still hadn't told him about Lacy.

When Madison returned downstairs, Ryan was in the kitchen. She could hear the sounds of cupboard doors being opened and cans and cartons sliding into the small compartments. She entered the kitchen, and Ryan turned immediately. "Are you all settled in?"

She cleared her throat. It was now or never. "Sort of."

"Well, you never *settle* in someone else's home. Best thing to do is think of this as a vacation lodge. You'll have plenty of time for reading and relaxing and walks in the woods, but even better," he said, smiling at her. Dimples appeared in his cheeks. His blue eyes sparkled. "There's a terrific stream about half a mile down the road. It has a waterfall," he said brightly, then shifted away again. "If you go there every day and relax, this really will be like a vacation for you."

When he went back to his groceries, Madison exhaled a breath she didn't realize she was holding. Something was going very wrong here. She wasn't supposed to find him attractive. It wasn't *wise* to find him attractive. They were trapped in this cabin for two weeks. Besides, big, rugged men weren't her type. Hell, let's face it, arrogant, bossy men weren't her type either. And that was more to the point. Yet when he smiled at her, her knees liquified.

Ryan continued to put groceries into the cupboards and Madison decided to help him, realizing that she could deliver her news about Lacy much more easily if her hands were busy and he was distracted. After assessing the storage system he was using, Madison picked up two cans and started toward the proper cupboard, but Ryan chose that same second to change his direction. They avoided a full-scale collision because Ryan raised his arms and slid by her. Unfortunately, he couldn't avoid touching her altogether. Their torsos brushed intimately and while Madison felt all the blood rush to her feet, she heard Ryan's quick indrawn breath.

"Excuse me," he said, quickly moving away from her.

She shook her head. "No, I'm sorry. I should have looked before I moved."

"Kitchen's a little cramped," Ryan said, stating the obvious. His voice was more husky than normal, and that was when Madison got her first clue that she wasn't the only one with the attraction problem. Her stomach tightened. This was a complication she didn't need. Her attraction to him was unexpected and unpredictable. Stranger than anything she'd ever experienced because it was as powerful as it was unexplainable....

She crossed that thought off. It wasn't unexplainable. It was very explainable. Ryan Kelly was gorgeous. He gave the term *sexy* its meaning. And though Madison normally wasn't attracted to blatantly sexy men, she was exceedingly attracted to this one—and he was attracted to her. Two worlds which never should have even intersected had just collided. The shots in the parking garage might have brought them together, but their magnetic pull caused the actual collision.

And they were stuck in this cabin for the next two weeks.

If he didn't have a problem with Lacy, they were in big trouble. Best to tell him about Lacy now before this thing went any further.

"Ryan, I..." she began, but the front door of the cabin opened.

"Yoo-hoo," Jessica called, "I brought you a present."

With his back to the kitchen door Ryan said, "Jessica, what are you doing here?" He turned then, saw the baby, and his mouth fell open.

Trying to see the scene the way Ryan would see it, Madison first took in tall, sophisticated Jessica, in her sleek black suit and her flawless chignon, appearing perfectly at home holding her pink bundle of joy. Dressed in a one-piece romper with a beret jauntily stretched over her head and one sprig of fine yellow hair sticking out on her forehead, Lacy looked cute enough to pose for one of the Kid-tastic ads, though Lacy would never see the front of any camera except Madison's. Tiny pink plaid tennis shoes covered her feet. She'd wrapped her legs around Jessica's waist.

"And what is *that?*"

"This," Jessica said, giving sleepy Lacy an affectionate bounce, "is Lacy."

Ryan didn't say another word. Astutely realizing that Jessica assumed Madison had told Ryan about Lacy, he focused his blue eyes on Madison and speared her with a glare that might have killed a lesser woman.

"Lacy's my daughter," Madison softly reported, as she lifted her chin defiantly. "I can't be without her for two weeks and she can't be without me. Besides, the only way we could be sure she'd be safe would be to keep her with me."

"Absolutely not," Ryan quietly said, then he went back to storing groceries as if closing the subject.

"You don't get a say here, Ryan," Jessica said, correctly interpreting the situation. "Madison is the witness. We are protecting the witness. Theoretically she gets what she wants. But more than that, the baby might need protection, too. If anybody finds out Madison has a child, Lacy would be the first target, not the last."

"*If anybody finds out,*" Ryan gasped, pivoting to face Jessica again. "I followed this woman around for two weeks and I never realized she had a child. I never had a damned inkling in two weeks of tracking the illustrious Ms. Delaney that she had a baby. And now, suddenly, you're worried somebody's going to find her?"

"It doesn't matter," Jessica returned.

"Like hell it doesn't!"

His last outburst scared Lacy and she broke into a screaming wail. Madison rushed over and slid her from

Jessica's arms, but even the comfort of her mother didn't quiet the baby. "I think I'd better take her upstairs and try to calm her down," Madison said, not the slightest bit sorry she had to miss this argument. Jessica would win, Madison knew that. She simply didn't want to hear the battle that would get them to the logical conclusion.

Madison left and Ryan rubbed his hand across the back of his neck. "I'm sorry, Jess, but this can't be done."

"Why not?"

"Why not?" he shouted, pivoting to face her again. "We're in the mountains for God's sake. There's never been a baby in this cabin. We're not equipped to accommodate one."

"Oh, Madison has everything a baby needs."

Ryan blew his breath out on a disgusted sigh. "I'm sure."

Bracing his arms against the sink, Ryan said, "I can't believe you didn't tell me. God, Jess, you know as well as I do that a child makes all the difference in the world when protecting a witness. Why the hell didn't you tell me?"

"Because no one knows about Lacy. Madison has gone to great lengths to keep Lacy a secret. And this was a prime example of why. If anyone had known Madison had a baby, Lacy would have been in danger. But more than that, Madison wants her child to have a normal life. I know about Lacy only because I'm Madison's best friend. So, though I have the power to assign her protection without telling her, I couldn't reveal a confidence I had because of our friendship."

"Peachy. We'll put you and Madison on *Oprah* and you can share your feelings with the world."

"Ryan, this is hardly the reaction I expected from you."

"Well, this is the reaction you're getting because whether you like it or not, whether you admit it or not, this *does* change everything."

Madison reentered the kitchen just as he said that. As a woman too long accustomed to being the leader, not an observer, she jumped into the conversation before she could remind herself this was Jessica's problem, not hers. "Why?" she asked, "Why does this change everything?"

Ryan whirled to face her. "We are in the mountains with a *baby* for God's sake. As far as I'm concerned that changes everything."

"I don't see how," Madison countered angrily. "I saw the way you drove up here. You know this mountain as well as I know my house. I also saw firsthand how good you are at protecting people." Realization struck and she paused, drew a long breath. "Jessica, would you mind leaving us alone for a minute?"

"If it'll solve the problem, no. Hell, no."

When Jessica was gone, Madison said, "Do you realize you're doing exactly what you accused your parents of doing?"

Ryan tossed her a confused look.

"You're expecting the world to be all adults."

He stared at her, then said, "You're crazy."

"I'm not crazy. Ten minutes ago you were telling me we were going to be fine. That I should think of myself as being on vacation. Then Jessica brings my child and suddenly everything's changed. We're not on vacation anymore, we're in grave danger and you can't handle me and a twenty-pound child." Her dander up, she marched over to stand in front of him. "Well, that's too bad because the world isn't made up of only adults. *My* world isn't made up of adults. I work with kids. I design for kids. I have a kid. Now you can either protect me as you promised, or you can go, but if you go, you're no better than your parents. You're simply a hypocrite since you won't admit it."

Obviously controlling his temper, he glanced away for a few seconds. The muscle in his jaw worked angrily. When he looked in her eyes, his blue orbs were like two white-hot laser beams. Her comment made him furious. The emotion in his eyes almost scared her.

In that second Madison realized they were connecting on a much deeper level than either expected they ever would. They'd gone from the superficial to the momentous in one quick conversation. He now knew her biggest secret, Lacy, but she also knew his. He didn't want to be compared to his parents.

Slowly, dangerously, he said, "I'm nothing like my parents." Then, almost as if making a dare or throwing down a gauntlet, he added, "I'll protect you and your child."

Chapter Four

Madison awakened to the sounds of birds singing. Startled, she bounced up in bed and glanced around. She saw the blue-and-red-plaid curtains, the rustic walls and oval rug and knew exactly where she was. A cool surge of emotion, part fear, part anger, rippled through her. Someone had shot at her, disrupted her life and, intentionally or not, threatened her child. She took a quick look to the right, and drew a long, satisfied breath. Curled in a ball, the bottom of her pink flannel pajamas angled skyward, Lacy lay in the Kidtastic top-of-the-line crib sleeping soundly.

Sleeping soundly? Lacy?

Curious, confused, Madison lifted the covers and rolled out of bed, cautiously making her way to the crib. As she stroked the fluffy yellow hair of her sleeping child, her brow furrowed. Her room was lit and pale sunlight peeked in between the separation of the plaid drapes, so she knew it was morning. But she didn't see a clock and had no idea of what time it was, or how late she'd slept. Just as that thought hit her, so did the smell of warm, succulent bacon. Her mouth watered.

In all the confusion she hadn't eaten the night before. Neither, she imagined, had Ryan Kelly.

They didn't speak at all after he agreed to guard her and Lacy. Instead he'd walked Jessica to her car, and Madison had taken advantage of that time to settle Lacy in. Then she'd grabbed a book from Angus's shelves with the purpose of entertaining herself while Lacy drifted to sleep, but Madison had drifted to sleep every bit as quickly.

Now, here they were. In exactly the same place they were the night before except she was starving and he was making breakfast. Her stomach rumbled. She hoped a good night's sleep had mellowed him, because she wasn't so foolish as to stay in her room when she was starving and delicious food sizzled only a few feet away. But she also wasn't in the mood to be yelled at or ignored or even bossed around. So he'd better be ready.

Madison didn't see the need to change her gray sweatshirt and fleece pants, merely added warm socks to her feet. She slapped a little water on her face, but decided against makeup or fixing her hair. She wasn't going to give this guy the wrong idea. They were trapped here. They didn't like each other. She had no intention of trying to get him to like her—which, if she remembered correctly, was part of their problem from the night before. They did share some sort of *physical* thing. But she didn't want to, and, she suspected, neither did he. One look at her attire and he'd see she didn't take her attraction to him any more seriously than she wanted him to take his attraction to her.

Satisfied that Lacy would continue to sleep peacefully, Madison padded from her bedroom, down the stairway, to the kitchen. At the doorway she didn't pause. She'd agreed to be a witness, it was his job to protect her. They were stuck, they would make the best of it.

Unfortunately, when she pushed open the door and saw

him standing at the stove with his back to her, she had her first ever set of second thoughts.

Dressed in only low-riding jeans and making her breakfast without qualm or complaint, this man was every woman's fantasy. Even without the breakfast, he was every woman's fantasy. She'd forgotten that. Their argument had blunted the memory of his shiny sandy brown hair, his brilliant blue eyes and his perfect body—a body she didn't have to guess about this morning. She could see he was well-muscled and spare. His broad shoulders tapered into a trim waist and tight hips.

She considered turning, going back to her room and waiting to see if maybe he'd eat and then dress completely, but she was hungry. Besides, after the way she'd accused him of being exactly like his parents, she could be almost certain she wouldn't hold any appeal for him this morning. If nothing else, Madison was reasonably sure their argument had cooled that completely.

And that suited her fine. Better than fine, actually.

Standing in the kitchen doorway, she cleared her throat to let him know she was behind him, then entered cautiously.

Ryan nearly dropped his bacon. Not because she'd scared him, but because she looked damned good. Luckily she spoke.

"Do you know how much cholesterol is in that food you're making?"

"Probably enough to give a less active man…person," he amended, slanting her a glance that took in everything from her hair to her fuzzy socks, "a heart attack. But I'm a very active person. I use all my cholesterol, thank you."

Turning back to the stove, he cursed himself for looking at her. Sleep-tousled, her bouncy blond hair was even sassier than normal, and though her eyes were heavy lidded and smoky they were still sharp, observant. Undoubtedly she'd noticed the way his gaze automatically skimmed over her, and he cursed himself again. He was drawn to her in a way he'd never been drawn to a woman before, and it was making him crazy, because there was no sense to it. Oh, sure, she was beautiful and sexy...no sensual. She wasn't sexy, she was sensual. And he was stopping this shopping list right now. He was supposed to be talking himself *out* of being attracted to her, not reenforcing his attraction by outlining all her good points. They were of such opposite dispositions and personalities that this attraction was nothing but an added problem. And, God help him, he'd better squelch it.

"Did you sleep well?" he asked, taking them to the most neutral conversational territory he could think of on short notice.

"Like a baby," she responded softly. "What time is it?"

"Six forty-five."

"Six forty-five!"

He grinned, deciding another glance to see the expression on her face couldn't hurt anything. "What's the matter? Not used to seeing the sun rise?"

"I normally awaken at five-thirty. Six forty-five is like sleeping in for me. But it feels much later. I mean I feel so rested. I had no idea an extra hour could make such a difference."

With the bacon done and the eggs fried to perfection, Ryan had no more reason to hide behind his duties. Holding one plate of eggs and one of bacon, he faced the breakfast bar. "You don't sleep in on weekends?" he asked, occupying himself with the inane conversation until he got himself accustomed to being face-to-face with this absolutely gorgeous, sleep warm woman who was snuggled into an oversize sweatshirt and gray fleece pants.

He stopped his thoughts. This was foolish. He was a trained professional, and he had a job to do and knew exactly how to do it. He knew how to distance himself and he *would* distance himself.

And she would never be any the wiser. In fact, she'd probably prefer his behaving in a professional way.

"Lacy sees to it that I never sleep in."

"That's right," he said, retrieving two plates from the cabinet beside the sink, grateful that this conversation could easily keep them in neutral ground. "I forgot you have a child."

The simple statement didn't insult, wasn't intended to. In fact, it was said with such a neutral tone it was almost an admission that he'd accepted Lacy. Madison relaxed and took the last few steps to the breakfast bar. She slid onto a stool. The good night's sleep seemed to have mellowed him.

Still cautious, she picked two strips of bacon from the serving dish and put them on her plate. "It's unusual she's sleeping this late this morning."

"You're going to find a lot of things will be different up here. Everything moves slower, easier. Both you and your daughter will get a very good rest if you let yourself. You'll go back to the city like new people."

Madison smiled in spite of herself. "I always thought buying a house in Crossroads Creek was country living. I had no idea how civilized our little town actually is."

"That's why Cal and Angus and I prefer the ranch. Small as Crossroads Creek is, it's still a town. And once a piece of land turns into a town, it loses something."

As he said the words, a fresh morning breeze filtered into the kitchen through the open window above the sink. It brought with it the scents of wildflowers and rich earth, which mingled with the aroma of fresh coffee and bacon. On the same sweet wave of air came the sounds of peace and tranquillity. A rustle of leaves, the chirp of a bird and nothing. Madison struggled not to close her eyes and savor.

"Hmm, you're right," she said absently, still caught up in the beauty of the morning.

"Coffee?"

"What? Yes," Madison said, brought out of her reverie. "I love coffee. I'm addicted to coffee."

He smiled. "That makes two of us."

Something tightened in Madison's chest. His was a companionable smile, and her reaction was nothing more than pleasure that she could be on the verge of making a new friend. But making friends with this man was something she never would have envisioned a few short hours ago. And, truthfully, she wasn't quite sure of the wisdom of such a friendship. She couldn't forget they were trapped in this cabin. Looking at his broad shoulders shimmering in the ray of sunlight flowing in through the wide kitchen window, she also couldn't forget just how physically attracted they were.

He poured a cup of coffee for her, and the ice around her resolve melted a little more. Never had she felt so comfortable, so relaxed with a perfect stranger. She had long-time business associates with whom she didn't feel completely calm. Yet, in less than twenty-four hours this man made her feel perfectly at ease with him.

Watching him return the coffeepot to the stove, Madison realized he was every bit as comfortable with her. After their arguments from the night before, it almost didn't make any sense.

Ryan took his seat again, and Madison immediately glanced down at the remainder of her uneaten food, pretending great interest so he wouldn't catch her staring at him. Luckily Lacy let out a screaming wail.

"That would be for me," Madison said, skirting her stool on her way out of the kitchen. Jogging up the steps, she drew a long, shuddering breath. *What the heck was all that?* she asked herself, then pushed open her bedroom door.

Lacy sat up in the crib, rubbing her eyes. Madison set to work to dress her for the morning, but as she did she couldn't stop thinking about what had happened between her and Ryan in the kitchen.

Logically, she could understand being physically tempted by him much more readily than she could understand liking him. Though, she realized as she unsnapped the inside of Lacy's one-piece pajamas, liking each other might not make sense, but being comfortable with each other was very explainable. Being forced into the situation last night where they both revealed their biggest secret had created a sort of intimacy. There was no pretense between them anymore. He was the first person with whom she could be a hundred percent comfortable about Lacy.

And she might be the first person around whom he didn't have to pretend about his parents.

No wonder their breakfast encounter was so peaceful.

Even if it was counterproductive.

Madison set Lacy in the tub, watched her eyes widen with delight as she skimmed her chubby hand through the bubbles, and knew Lacy was part of the reason she shouldn't make too much out of this. Comfortable or not, Ryan couldn't sweep his initial reaction to Lacy under the rug. He may have different reasons from his parents, but he obviously didn't like kids. He also made it perfectly clear that he didn't approve of Madison's lifestyle. This few weeks in the cabin might be a respite of sorts for both of them, but the real world still existed. And in the real world, he wouldn't want her or her baby.

After Lacy was dressed in jeans and a sweatshirt, Madison carried her to the kitchen to make her breakfast. The look on Ryan's face when she pushed through the swinging door wiped away any question she had about his feelings about children.

She didn't know whether to breathe a sigh of relief or be disappointed, but she did know simply from the way he stiffened and the way his eyes narrowed when he looked at Lacy, that making too much of this attraction between them wasn't merely foolish, it was downright wrong.

Chapter Five

Madison hadn't taken two steps into the kitchen before Ryan knew everything had changed. Not only did the baby make him nervous, but now he was back to dealing with the CEO of Kidtastic and not the woman he was supposed to be protecting. Part of him admitted disappointment. The other part relaxed. There was simply too much chemistry between them for them to get too close, too comfortable with each other.

"Should I make her something to eat?" he asked stupidly because he really didn't know.

"No," Madison briskly replied. "Lacy's going to have cereal."

"I don't know if we brought cereal."

"*You* may not have brought cereal," Madison announced efficiently as she balanced her child on her hip and slid the multicolored plastic high chair from the corner in which Jessica had stored it the night before. "But cereal was at the top of Jessica's list of things for me."

"You know," Ryan said, leaning against the cupboard

to appear casual, though his brain was running about a thousand miles a second as he drew some confusing conclusions. "You talked with Jessica on the phone. You knew Jessica was meeting us up here. You had Jessica packing things for the baby. Why didn't you have her bring *you* some clothes? Why did you borrow things from Grace?"

Putting Lacy into the high chair, Madison spared him a glance. "Because Lacy wasn't at my house, and I didn't want to impose upon Jessica to go there."

"Then how did Jessica get Lacy's things?"

"She has extra of everything she needs at her nanny's."

"She *goes* to her nanny, the nanny doesn't come to her?"

"Mr. Kelly, I've spent Lacy's entire life keeping her hidden from the press and the public. Having child care away from my house is part of my strategy."

"Which explains why you've got double of everything—all of which can be packed at a moment's notice."

"Exactly. I'm used to making alternative plans for Lacy. I know what to do when we're forced to travel separately. Getting her up here wasn't a hardship."

Not about to be duped, he shook his head. "I'm not buying it. Oh, I mean, I agree that you might have an outside baby-sitter and I believe you also have doubles of everything Lacy needs at her baby-sitter's house. But I don't think you were *forced* to travel separately."

Stirring Lacy's cereal, Madison smiled skeptically. "Would you have gone back to get Lacy if I'd asked?"

"If Jessica would have instructed me to get Lacy, I wouldn't have had a choice. Jessica knows that. So there's a reason we brought different cars."

Sighing, Madison peered up from fixing Lacy's breakfast. "Why does it bother you?"

"It doesn't bother me. I *need* to know. I need to know

exactly what I'm dealing with here. So tell me why we came in two vehicles.''

She sighed again and started feeding the gurgling baby. ''Because there was a very real possibility that I could have been killed last night driving to the cabin.''

''And you didn't want the baby with you if you were killed.''

''I didn't want the baby with *us*,'' she qualified, busily feeding her daughter. Ryan noticed that Madison was quick, efficient with the job, and realized that could only be because she'd had plenty of practice. Lacy might have nannies, but from a few minutes of watching Madison, it was obvious Lacy's mother was her primary care giver.

''Do you know how easily someone could have shot you when you were driving, which meant the car would have been wrecked and both of us would have been killed?''

''Along with the baby.''

She nodded. ''Along with the baby.''

''So you were protecting her?''

Visibly annoyed, she set the spoon in the mushy cereal. ''What difference does it make?''

''It makes a great deal of difference because I'm wondering if there isn't a thin line between protecting and hiding.''

She gaped at him. ''Of course I'm hiding her! Good God, I came right out and told you that. And if you're trying to find the big mystery here, save yourself some trouble. I'm hiding this child to give her a normal life. I don't want her confused by the glare of the spotlight. But most of all I don't want her subjected to the public speculation about who her father might be. In other words, I don't want her to take the brunt of gossip for a choice *I* made.''

She paused long enough to get a breath. ''Come hell or

high water, Sheriff Kelly, I plan to see this child has a normal life.''

Turning away, Ryan ran his hand over his mouth. He knew it was his career in law enforcement that had him mistrusting her motives, the only thing he couldn't figure out was why. Why he cared. The woman was perfect. Beautiful. Successful. Personable. And now a good mother. A terrific mother.

Watching her feeding her gurgling baby, Ryan had to admit that that was the problem. She *was* perfect. She impressed the hell out of him, and he was searching for a flaw because he didn't want her to impress him. He *wanted* to dislike her. Disliking her would make this next two weeks much easier.

She wiped a smudge of cereal from her baby's happy face, and Ryan leaned against the counter again, crossing his arms on his chest. While she'd gone upstairs for Lacy, he'd changed into a plaid shirt and put on his boots, but she'd stayed in her sweatpants and fuzzy socks. Yet she still looked absolutely adorable. There's was no doubt about it. She didn't have a flaw.

He watched her coo at her daughter. She was an especially faultless mother...a wonderful, attentive, gentle mother. But then again, what did he expect from a woman whose company was called Kidtastic.

Madison's company was one of the new wave of manufacturers that didn't merely create clothes, car seats, high chairs, toys and every other ancillary article kids needed. Her company also created an attitude about kids. Discipline with love that translated into bright but safe toys, and colorful but practical clothes.

Staring at happy, bouncy Lacy, sitting in a comfortable contraption as colorful as the Fourth of July, and dressed in a one-piece garment made of cheerfully striped material that bent and stretched with her, Ryan realized Madison certainly practiced what she preached. It appeared that Lacy used every product Madison produced for kids. And she used them well and contentedly, physically proving Madison's theories about child rearing.

Ryan shook his head, thinking how jealous his father would have been of the genius of this woman. Lord knows that if Graham Kelly could have found a way to use his only child to enhance his business, he certainly would have done it...

Ryan looked at Lacy, then at Madison, then at Lacy again. *That was it!* That was the damned connection that had been bugging him all morning. This ultra-successful manufacturer of everything from diapers to car seats had a baby. *A secret baby.* It could very well be true that she wanted to shield her child from the glare of her spotlight. But, it made a hell of a lot more sense that she'd rather hide her competitive edge. All really successful people had a competitive edge. And most of them hid it—Ryan knew that firsthand from his father—and Miss Madison Delaney, entrepreneur and author was hiding hers.

That thought absolutely infuriated him, but when he took his analysis one step further and wondered if she hadn't actually *had* her child to give herself a competitive edge, Ryan knew he had to leave the room.

Walking toward the kitchen door, Ryan said, "I think I'll check the grounds."

Confused, Madison glanced over. He'd been quiet for so long that she'd almost forgotten he was there. One look at his face, though, and she knew that was probably for the best. Anger etched itself into his furrowed brow. His blue eyes were as cool as the Arctic. "Why don't you pick up a gallon of rocky road ice cream while you're out?" she teased, knowing they were too far from civilization for him to do that, but hoping he'd see the humor in their situation and lighten up a bit.

He glared at her. "You do know on some level or another that you can't have everything that you want?"

Stunned by the intensity of his tone, Madison reined in her own temper and smiled tentatively. "Sorry. That was a joke."

"Yeah, right," he said and grabbed the doorknob.

But something pulled him back and turned him around again. Madison could almost see him try to stop his next comment and fail.

"You know, my father would have been very proud of you. Not everybody's smart enough to figure out she actually has to live with a baby to be able to design for babies. You're one hell of a smart cookie, you know that, right up there with the best of them."

He slammed the door when he left the cabin and Madison sat back on her seat, while Lacy slapped her round hands on the tray of her high chair.

Well, that answered about fifty-seven questions about what the hell he'd been thinking the whole time she'd fed Lacy and he'd stared at her as if doing calculus in his head. Infuriated, she rose and rummaged in a diaper bag until she found a cloth to dampen for cleaning her child. Not only had he been comparing her to his parents, but it sounded like she'd come up even more selfish than he considered *them* to be. All because he had the outrageous notion that she used Lacy in her work.

Of all the stupid, imbecilic…

Sliding Lacy from the high chair, Madison reminded herself that the real problem here was that Ryan Kelly jumped to conclusions. She'd seen it last night. He didn't understand why she'd refused protection, so he assumed she was addle-brained. Then he made the connection that since she was successful, she must be like his parents. Now, he'd decided that since she had a child about the age of the children for whom she designed, she used her child like a guinea pig.

Which was absurd...particularly since the timing of using Lacy as a guinea pig didn't work. If he'd take minute to think about it, he'd realize her company was much older than her child, and his insult was way off base.

He was, she decided with unqualified authority, an idiot.

When Ryan returned two hours later, Lacy was in the crib napping. Angry, and not wanting to be, because she didn't want his behavior to affect her so powerfully, Madison tried to ignore him when he came in the front door. But it was no use. She wasn't used to anyone treating her like this, and though she wouldn't dignify his insult with an explanation, she did have an issue with his competency, an issue she felt she had every right to address since he had her life and her child's life in his hands.

"I just have one little question," she said sarcastically as he entered the main room and tossed his hat on a convenient peg. "Exactly how are you protecting me and my child when you go for two-hour walks?"

He grunted, making his way into the kitchen. "That trip around the perimeter was necessary to assure your safety. Now that I've checked things out, I know no one's within five miles. There are no campfires, no vehicles, no tracks. I needed to be certain no one followed us."

She scrambled off the couch. "Yeah, right. You needed to be certain no one followed us," she repeated, mocking him. "There is no way anyone followed us."

"You don't know that."

"Oh, come on," she gasped, grabbing his arm to spin him around when he would have turned away from her. "We're perfectly safe and you know it. And all while you were out playing Barnie Fife, I did the dishes and dusted the living room."

For several seconds he simply stared at her. He glanced down where her fingers gripped the sleeve of his plaid shirt, then brought his gaze back to her face again.

"If this little argument is all about me not helping with the dishes, you can save your breath. I know where my responsibilities lie. I'll take care of what I have to take care of when it needs taken care of."

Her eyes narrowed. "Oh, you'd rather live in a pigsty?"

Ryan stepped back, away from the light touch of her fingers on his sleeve, confused by why she was angry, but more confused about why he was still attracted to her even though she was being ridiculous.

"That's it," she ranted, obviously furious. "Walk away. Don't talk about this. God knows we wouldn't want to actually face a problem when we can walk away."

"What are you talking about?"

"About you, you idiot," she yelped, marching over to him again. Before he realized what was happening, her scent found his nostrils, the gleam in her amber eyes caught and intrigued him, and her words seemed to float into oblivion. She was without a doubt one sexy woman. Even ranting—or maybe because anger had her expressing herself to the fullest—she was exquisite...passionate. That was it. Passionate. She didn't do things by half measures, and like her or not, approve of her or not, he found her energy arousing. Incredibly arousing. Dangerously arousing.

When she realized she didn't have his attention, there was no light brush of her fingers on his forearm. This time she jabbed her index finger in his chest. Something inside of Ryan snapped. His closely guarded control was set free and beneath it lay nothing but pure sensation and greed. Grabbing her forearms, he hoisted her up to his height, then he lowered his head and dropped his mouth to hers.

Madison expected a reaction from Ryan, but not the weight of his mouth pressed against hers. She expected fire.

But not this. Never this. How was a person supposed to
react sanely, when her knees had liquified and every muscle
in her body was straining forward instead of pulling away?
For a giddy instant, she stood frozen, immobile, then instinct took over and she kissed him back. She let her fingers
tunnel into the hair at his nape, let her arms rest on his
broad shoulders, let her breasts cushion into his chest. He
was right, she realized hazily. Very, very right. Arguing
wouldn't settle what was wrong with them. And kissing
was only the first step.

Drugged, pliant, she accepted the suckling caresses of
his mouth, let her head fall back, let him take her where
he would.

Chapter Six

As if in slow motion, Ryan pulled away. Stunned, aroused, Madison blinked up at him. Damp and dewy, her lips tingled. Her body hummed with need. She saw a reflection of that need in Ryan's Mediterranean blue eyes, but as quickly as she saw it, he banked that need, drew back and set her away from him.

"Sorry," he said, then rubbed his hand across the back of his neck. "I'm not exactly sure why I did that."

Madison blinked again, confused because she'd thought she knew exactly why he'd done that. He'd done it because he got tired of fighting the attraction, and he'd given in. If he hadn't kissed her for that reason and wasn't sure why he'd kissed her, then she'd misinterpreted everything. He might have actually kissed her because she looked like she was asking for it.

Mortified, she took a pace back. "Don't apologize," she said, shamed when her voice quavered. "Let's just forget it happened."

"Forget it happened?" Ryan asked incredulously, then

ran his hand along the back of his neck again. Ten minutes ago, while walking through the forest, he'd all but convinced himself that he disliked this woman enough to request that Jessica send his deputy to the cabin to guard her. But one taste of her honeyed lips and he was imagining things he hadn't dreamed of in years, remembering fantasies he'd believed to be nothing but wicked dreams, and considering possibilities that made his blood so hot he wondered how he'd found the control to set her away from him. "How the hell do you forget something like that?"

"As my guardian, Sheriff Kelly, you'd better figure that out very quickly, or I won't have any choice but to call Jessica and request another officer."

Though he'd considered the same thing only a few minutes before, Ryan stiffened with indignation. "There's no need for that."

"See that there isn't," she said, her spine ramrod straight, her yellow-brown eyes so cool he thought the furnace might kick on.

Ryan didn't know what the hell was going on here, but he did know that he didn't even want to *like* this woman, yet kissing her had been better than skydiving, mountain climbing and skiing all put together. It didn't make any sense but, then again, it didn't have to. His only purpose was to protect her for the next two weeks, then get her safely to the trial. That was it. End of story.

"You won't have anything to worry about from me," he said and tried to turn away from her, but she called him back.

"You won't kiss me again," she insisted, her amber eyes skewering him with a hard, cold stare.

He almost cursed, but caught himself. Capturing her gaze, he wondered how eyes such a warm color could appear so cold, so ruthless. "I said it won't happen again. I keep my word."

"See that you do," she crisply stated, and walked toward the steps. "I'm going to check on Lacy."

When she was gone, Ryan let out his breath in a long whoosh. Though she'd said she was checking on Lacy, he knew she'd find something else upstairs to occupy her and wouldn't be back. He wasn't sure if she was punishing him, or giving both of them a chance to cool off. Whatever her reasoning, staying out of sight for a while was definitely for the best, because though she no longer had to worry about him kissing her, strangling her was beginning to look mighty appealing.

Restless, angry, he roamed the main room for a few minutes, glancing at book titles, considering another walk, then eyeing the portable phone. Inspired, he plopped himself into an overstuffed chair and dialed the number for the ranch. After several rings Cal answered.

"Nobody else must be home."

"You got that right," Cal said, and though his voice was gruff and irritated, Ryan knew that was only because he had to answer the phone, not because he didn't wish to speak with Ryan.

"What's up?"

"This is a ranch, Ryan," Cal said, sounding exasperated. "Nothing new happens here. You're the one with the life, Mr. Big-Time Sheriff," he continued with brotherly exasperation. "You're also guarding a witness for an important trial. If anybody's got news around here, it should be you. What's up with Madison Delaney?"

Only that he'd kissed her, Ryan thought then scowled deeply. "Nothing."

"Well, that ends yet another male-bonding session."

"Gee, Cal, thanks for the support."

"If something's wrong," Cal prodded, and in his mind's eye Ryan could see him take a seat on the old leather chair in Angus's office and, uncaring, throw his booted feet on a stack of paperwork. "You've got to tell me. I'm not a clairvoyant like Grace or Angus."

"All right, all right," Ryan groused, then ran his hand down his face, debating. In the end he knew he'd called home because he wanted to talk with someone. Cal was actually the best option. "I'm really attracted to this woman, Cal. And it's driving me nuts."

To add insult to injury, Cal laughed heartily. "Angus and I warned you."

"I know you did. Hell, I warned myself. But that doesn't help it or stop it. I need advice. Good, sound advice."

"Why?"

"Why?" This time Ryan did swear. "For God's sake, I'm supposed to be guarding her, not fantasizing about her."

"Why?"

"I'm going to come through this phone and slap you."

"Because I won't let you off the hook?" Cal asked pleasantly. "If you like this woman, go after her."

Realizing Cal was serious, Ryan scrubbed his hand down his face again. "It's not that simple."

"I can't see why not."

"For God's sake, Cal, aside from the obvious, there's absolutely no reason for me to be attracted to her. She's in the public eye more than my parents were. And in her own way, I think she's even more ambitious, even more cool and calculating than Graham and Althea could ever have been."

There was a long pause before Cal quietly said, "Coming from you, that's quite an insult."

"It is," Ryan agreed and began to pace. "She has a child," Ryan said, confiding in Cal only because he knew what he said would go no further. "A little girl not quite a year old. She hides her, she said, to protect her and to give her a normal life."

"That's sort of noble."

"It would be, if I believed it. But something about this situation bugged me all night and all morning. While I was watching her feed the baby it hit me that the odd little coincidence is that Madison designs for babies, writes about babies, creates everything creatable for babies...and—surprise—she has a baby."

"So, she has an inside track."

"You don't find that a little convenient?"

"For whom?"

"For her. God, Cal. She has a baby and she hides her. Why would she hide Lacy except that she doesn't want the world to know she used her own child to make herself successful?"

Another long pause followed that statement. Finally Cal said, "Have you been nipping at Angus's Scotch?"

"I hate Scotch."

"Well, something's addling your brain. Everybody this side of Houston knows Madison Delaney has been CEO of Kidtastic for over six years. Started her company right out of college when she was running a day care center. She didn't use that kid to make herself rich and famous. She made herself rich and famous all by herself—and years before she had her own child."

Heat rushed from Ryan's feet the whole way to his temples. Which was actually a better place for it than where it usually was when he thought about Madison. It was no wonder he'd screwed up. He'd forgotten real people think with their brains. "God, I made an ass of myself on that one."

Laughter filled Cal's voice. "I'll bet you did." He paused. "So now you don't have any reason not to pursue her."

Ryan scrubbed his hand over his mouth. "I have plenty of reason. She's still a workaholic. Something—*some-*

one—gets neglected in her life, and since she's not married, it's fairly obvious which end of her life gets the short stick.''

To Ryan's utter mortification, Cal chortled with glee. ''Do you realize you're thinking in terms of happily ever after—not a quick fling, not even dating—with this woman?''

Ryan said nothing.

Voice laced with laughter, Cal said, ''Ryan, my boy, you are in trouble. Big, big trouble.''

Irritated, Ryan hung up the phone, knowing Cal was way off base. He was not in trouble. Not at all. Not even a little bit.

Unfortunately, when Madison walked down the stairs dressed in blue jeans and a sweater, her yellow hair caught in a loose ponytail at the top of her head, looking better than most women looked dressed to go out on the town, Ryan realized Cal was right. He *was* in trouble. Big, big trouble.

Knowing he had to get hold of himself, Ryan took a seat on the overstuffed chair again and reached for a magazine. ''I can start lunch anytime you'd like.''

She eyed him suspiciously. He almost winced, knowing he deserved it. ''I don't usually eat a big lunch.''

''Don't have to,'' he said, raising his eyes from his reading. They flicked quickly from top to bottom, taking in and admiring everything from her curly ponytail to her stocking-covered feet. ''If you want you can just have a sandwich.''

Madison felt the knots forming in her stomach. She hadn't missed his inventory any more than she'd missed making her own as she walked down the steps. It was hard not to stare when someone was put together as perfectly as he was. Jeans and a scruffy plaid shirt highlighted his rugged masculinity. His light brown hair curled naturally, sexily around his collar. His blue eyes didn't miss a thing, even as they revealed everything he was thinking. "A sandwich would be fine."

"Fine."

"Good."

The conversation died a quick, natural death, and though Madison knew she should have been glad not to have to communicate with this man, another part of her wished they could wade through this awkwardness. But it wasn't going to happen. Knowing he didn't like the way she'd chosen to live her life was worse than thinking he didn't like her child. Eventually, everybody warmed up to Lacy. It was easy to recognize his feelings could change. But there was no way in hell he'd warm up to her lifestyle.

And no way in hell she'd change.

Chapter Seven

Madison and Ryan actually got through the next two days by avoiding each other. Lacy created the perfect diversion for Madison, who found she could use her daughter as a buffer when Lacy was awake, and, when Lacy was sleeping, she could read, sitting on the chair by her crib. Meals were short and quiet. Ryan cooked, Madison ate. She ate with verve and purpose, and a single-minded dedication to get back to her room.

Unfortunately, on the third day, Madison started to soften toward him, because he seemed to anticipate her needs as if he could read her mind. There was something decadently satisfying about having an unreasonably handsome man cook you the perfect breakfast, make coffee ten minutes before you realized you wanted it and keep the bathroom stocked with fresh towels.

She almost felt shrewish and rude for staying away from him, then she remembered their attraction and that he didn't like her lifestyle, and she pulled back into her shell again. It didn't matter how many times he turned her knees to jelly with the meaningful gleam in his potent blue eyes. She could ignore him. She had to. They were not a match made in heaven. The minute either one of them spoke, they were fighting. Hence, she stayed quiet. Very quiet. So quiet the sounds of the forest around them provided perpetual background music.

That strategy could have and should have taken them the whole way to the trial, except Madison was accustomed to working hard for nine or ten hours every day. A three-day respite had been good for her soul and psyche, but on the fourth day she wished for a computer with the same passion and desperation as she'd wished for a cigarette the day after she'd quit smoking.

She ambled down the stairs, and in one quick glance, Ryan knew there was going to be trouble. There was a brightness about her eyes that reminded him of a lion—a mother lion hunting food for her cub. Her muscles were tight, her movements were stiff, restricted. When she looked at him, Ryan could swear she didn't see him.

He closed the novel he was reading. "Something wrong?"

She cleared her throat and smiled sheepishly. Ryan's stomach tightened, all his senses went on red alert. He hadn't forgotten she tempted him beyond belief, though he didn't think four days of control could be tossed out the window this quickly. Using her smile was a dirty trick. A mean trick. The woman was definitely up to no good.

"You wouldn't happen to have a portable computer lying around anywhere, wouldn't you?"

He almost laughed, but caught himself, not wanting to antagonize her. "Nope. No computer. Sorry."

Glancing around with quiet desperation, Madison said, "With everything else Angus has in this place, surely it's not impossible that he'd have one simple portable PC."

Taking pity, Ryan smiled. "Going through withdrawal?"

She sighed, fell to the sofa. "In a big, big way. I haven't wanted anything this much since my last cigarette craving."

"Well, we don't have any cigarettes, either, but Angus has a nice stash of cigars."

"Oh, that would be great. It took me a whole year to quit smoking. Nothing like starting up again but this time with cigars. That would be a lesson for Lacy."

"Well, we're going to have to get you something," Ryan pointed out logically, as he rose from his seat. He'd seen this before. Witness boredom, day four. Right on schedule, actually.

"I'd settle for a legal pad and a crayon right now."

"You go get a crayon from Lacy's cache of toys and I'll dig around for the legal pad."

He said it easily, comfortably, and Madison almost relaxed. Almost. No matter what he said or what he did, he couldn't get rid of that predatory gleam in his brilliant blue eyes. Or the tension that coiled through him, giving him the look of a man about to pounce. And, God help her, she couldn't stop her reaction to it. He was tight and strained. She was tingles and puddling softness, fighting a magnetic pull that constantly urged her to stand closer, talk softer, wrap herself around him and see what happened. They were a pair. A sad, disgusting pair of lunatics who couldn't get hold of their hormones.

"Let's see," he said, striding to the kitchen. "If I were a legal pad, where would I be?"

"Beside the phone," Madison said, and rushed to the end table holding the portable. She yanked open the single drawer, but found it empty.

"Strike one," Ryan said from the kitchen, as if he'd seen her, though Madison knew he hadn't. "Angus comes up here to rest and relax. He typically doesn't bring the cellular phone. That's how I know there wouldn't be a legal pad in that drawer."

She scowled at the kitchen wall. Did he always have to be right?

"But he would have to create a shopping list if he decided to stay longer than he'd planned. Which means he might have a pad in one of these drawers."

As he spoke, Madison could hear the sounds of drawers opening and closing. He didn't rummage through them, obviously he didn't have to. He opened them one after another as if he found each empty and moved on to the next.

"Okay, now we know there's none in the kitchen, either," he announced, entering the main room. A beam of sunlight shrouded him and Madison cursed softly under her breath. Why in the hell did he have to look so wonderful, and why in the hell was she so wickedly attracted to him? She wasn't a weak woman, she was a strong woman. A vital, strong, intelligent, emotionally satisfied CEO of a huge company. What in the hell was happening to her?

"Where does that leave us?" she asked, her voice gruff and angry, and she didn't care. She was desperate to work and tired of being drawn to a man who considered her to be worse than the parents he hated.

"Now, now, don't give up hope yet," he said, soothing her. Though under normal circumstances, his calm words might have made her feel churlish, today she felt she had every right to be irritable. In fact, she clung to her anger. That was far, far better than being soft and mellow around him because that only got her into trouble.

Ryan dug through the books on the bookshelves, opened the drawers of the end tables and finally found a legal pad under one of the overstuffed chairs.

"Aha!" he crowed triumphantly as he rose from behind the chair, waving the legal pad and a stick pen.

She could have kissed him. Not because she was unreasonably attracted to him, but because she was grateful for the pen and paper. She grabbed them from his hands and rounded the sofa, not looking when she dropped onto the puffy cushion. As if the sight of the writing instruments had clicked on her brain, she wrote feverishly, passionately.

She was aware that Ryan took the seat across from her and watched her as she wrote. She didn't care, and he didn't interfere with her speeding thoughts. She wrote and wrote until, as abruptly as they'd begun, her ideas stopped.

Exhausted, she fell against the back of the sofa. "Whew."

"I'm tired, and all I did was watch," Ryan admitted carefully. "Do you know you've been writing for twenty minutes?"

She glanced over at him. "That's all? Sometimes I can go like that for over an hour...but then, I have a computer and it's much easier to get all your ideas, before they get away from you."

"That's amazing."

Laughing a little, she shook her head. "No, it's not. It's all part of being creative."

"I never thought of your job as being creative."

"Who do you think comes up with all the ideas for new products?"

"Well, you do," he said slowly, again cautiously, then he threw his hands up in resignation, rose and began to pace. "Look, I'm tired of skirting the obvious," he said uncomfortably. "I'm tired of us avoiding each other, or talking like idiots when we do try to make conversation. So, I'm going to apologize for what I said to you the other morning."

"I'm not quite sure I know what you mean," she said, though she knew exactly what he meant. What she wasn't quite sure about was whether or not she wanted to discuss it again. Regardless of the fact that he wasn't a hundred percent happy, they did have something of a truce going here. It would be a shame to ruin it with an honest conversation.

"I'm talking about backhandedly accusing you of using Lacy for research."

"I do use Lacy for research...now. Up until seven months ago I didn't have her, and—"

"And you made it on your own. I know. But I insinuated a hell of a lot more than that you used Lacy for research." He drew a long breath, mercifully not embarrassing her or infuriating her by expanding on his insinuation. "I was cruel and thoughtless, and I'm sorry."

"Apology accepted," Madison said, though now it was her turn to be uncomfortable, because his apology wasn't merely sweet and considerate, it also wasn't easy for him. So, she had to be a lady and accept it. But being angry with each other had actually worked very well to keep them apart. She wasn't sure it would be wise for them to get friendly again. Unfortunately she also wasn't sure how to get out of the room quickly and gracefully.

"What did you write?" he asked, moving to sit right beside her on the couch.

She stiffened. "Basically, only notes."

"What kind of notes?" he asked, then reached for her legal pad.

She clutched it tightly. "Just goofy things that came to mind while we were here."

"What kind of things could you possibly think about here?"

She gave him an exasperated look. "Things that would make it easier for parents to take their babies camping."

"Oh," he said, understanding. "Having a baby does help you."

"In a way," she admitted with a shrug, growing comfortable with him again in spite of her attempts not to. "But

I'd like to think I would have come up with a lot of these things on my own, even without Lacy.''

"Maybe," he agreed amicably.

"Maybe," she repeated, not sure what else to say.

"I'm still not making the connection of how a single woman could develop such a successful child care company. I know you had the day care center, but why? What would make a single person want to take care of kids?"

Debating, she drew a long breath, and concluded it couldn't hurt to talk about something as generic as how she created her company. "I have a degree in business, but didn't have any product in particular I wanted to manufacture and market, so I decided I'd take the elementary road."

"The elementary road?"

"Well, every city, town, borough, or even a group of houses has a need for baby-sitting services. Which makes it elementary that if you provide those services you have an instant business."

"Makes sense," he said, laying his arm across the back of the sofa.

Equal and opposite reactions pummeled Madison. Half of her screamed a warning of danger. The other half nearly leaned into the nook created by his arm.

"But it doesn't explain how you got into the manufacturing business."

She cleared her throat. "Well, I owe that to being lazy."

Ryan laughed. His deep, rich baritone filled the main room of the cabin. "Excuse me?"

"I got my best ideas from creating little things to help me make my job as day care provider easier."

"You mean you actually took care of the kids?"

"Who else was going to?" Madison asked incredulously. "I only brought in enough money from my clients to pay for the house we used, to buy the materials and supplies we needed and to pay my salary and the salary of one aide.

"Expansion was bringing in another child. But before you could bring in another child you had to be sure you could care for that child. So, I started creating things that would help us do our jobs, like chairs that were easier to use and *safer*...because liability insurance can be a killer."

"And one day the parent of one of your children saw one of your inventions and helped you start your business," Ryan speculated knowingly.

She shook her head. "No, one day I woke up and realized I would be spending the rest of my life struggling if I didn't soon think of something. What I decided to do was to patent a few of my ideas and sell the use of those patents to a manufacturer. I took the money I got from that and financed the company I run now."

"All because you didn't want to run a day care anymore."

She shook her head again. "All because I didn't want to be poor anymore."

"There's no shame in being poor," Ryan said, watching her.

She stared at him. "Really? Have you tried it?"

"Yes and no..."

"There is no 'yes and no' about being poor, either you've been there or you haven't. If you're not quite sure, then you haven't."

"Which makes me unacceptable in your eyes?"

The absurdity of the situation appealed to her. She smiled. "In a roundabout way, yes."

"That's interesting, a workaholic who doesn't like me because I've never been poor."

There was just enough insult in his tone to get her dander up. "I never said I didn't like you. But since we're hitting this subject like a ten-penny nail, let's really hit it. The problem isn't that I don't like you, it's that I don't want to have anything to do with you. And I don't want anything to do with you because you're sanctimonious.''

''Sanctimonious?''

''Yes. You're sure you're right and sure anybody who doesn't agree with you is wrong. You're especially convinced you know everything about me. But the truth is you don't have a clue about where I've come from, or what motivates me to work as hard as I do. My guess is you also don't have a clue about what motivated your parents, either. You'd much rather sit back and criticize.''

''Let's keep my parents out of this.''

''No,'' she said, standing to get away from him. ''You don't like me...or don't *want* to like me because I remind you of your parents, when the reality is...''

He caught her wrist so quickly, Madison didn't realize he'd moved. ''I think you've got the theories and definitions a little confused,'' he said. ''Or maybe the people. It seems to me that you're the one who's talking as if she knows about something when she doesn't. You talk about my not understanding what it's like to be poor, but can you understand what it's like to be alone...really alone—*completely* alone—when you're nine years old? Too young to find your own friends and too old for the nanny to entertain. So you sit in your room day in and day out...by yourself for years.'' He shook his head as if trying to rid himself of unwanted thoughts. ''No, you can't imagine what it's like. Most people can't.'' He paused, considered, then added, ''But I'll bet Lacy can...or at least she will.''

''How dare you!''

''I dare because I know. You can't judge me, Madison, because you *don't* know. And what makes you angry about me isn't that I always think I'm right, but that you can see I *am* right. I *have* been there. I *have* done that. And it upsets you to have me point out to you what a mistake you're making with your child. And that's actually what's bugging you.''

Anger had her blood boiling. It was difficult to get a breath. Madison struggled for enough air to let him have it, but good.

He beat her to the punch. "Save whatever it is you think you have to say. I'm going out.''

"Where?" Madison demanded.

"I don't know and I don't care. All I know is that it's best for you and me to spend more time away from each other than together.''

Chapter Eight

A loud wail awakened Madison, and she bounced up in bed, knowing the cry was Lacy's but also not wanting to have that cry awaken their not-quite-hospitable host. After their most recent argument, the last thing she wanted was to have to explain or apologize for the fact that her child cried.

Scrambling to the crib, Madison acknowledged that Ryan's unhappy childhood had left him bitter and angry, and part of her actually agreed he had a right to all of those emotions. What she didn't agree with was the way he kept taking his anger out on her. Oh, she knew she reminded him of things he'd wanted to keep locked away, things he didn't want to remember. Maybe even things he didn't want to face. But that wasn't her fault. It wasn't his. It wasn't anybody's. And they still had over a week to stay together in this cabin.

Madison reached in and pulled Lacy from the crib, cradling her against her bosom, but instead of being comforted, Lacy simply screamed all the louder. Which was a sign of one thing.

Teething.

Running her finger along the inside of Lacy's gums, Madison felt the little bumps and ridges that indicated a new tooth was attempting to sprout, and she sighed. Great. Exactly what they needed.

Praying that Jessica had had the foresight to pack the medicine, Madison carried her crying child to the dresser where she'd stored Lacy's things. After rummaging for a few minutes, she blew her hair out of her eyes. Jessica wasn't married, she was a career woman whose single exposure to a child was Lacy. She couldn't be expected to think of teething, let alone to think of packing the medicine to numb her gums. And Madison couldn't have been expected to remind Jessica to bring the medicine since being shot at hadn't put her at her motherly best the night she told Jessica to bring Lacy to the cabin.

Snuggling her sobbing child, Madison knew they'd awaken Sir Dragon Temper if they didn't do something, but at this point, the only thing Madison could think to do was take Lacy downstairs and rub her gums with ice. All things being considered, it was better than nothing.

Muffling Lacy's sobs against her bosom in order not to disturb Ryan, Madison whisked Lacy from their room and down the steps in record time. She didn't turn on a light until they were in the kitchen. Still cradling Lacy against her bosom to muffle her cries, she grabbed the ice, wrapped it in a paper towel and carried her child into the main room, where she settled them on the sofa. When she pulled Lacy away from her breast, Lacy's wails provided the perfect opportunity to slide the ice into her mouth, and the suddenness of the move instantly silenced her.

Madison took advantage of Lacy's acquiescence and glided the ice along her gums. Though she whimpered, Lacy actually stayed fairly still. Calmed, Madison leaned back against the cushions. Seeking to really relax while

Lacy numbed her gums, Madison put her feet on the low table, but, because the room was dark, she didn't see the soda can Ryan had left the night before and sent it careening into the darkness.

It hit the floor and bounced so many times it sounded like a marching band tuning up before a football game. Madison heard Ryan's door burst open and the sound of his feet pounding down the hall. In a matter of seconds, he flew into the main room, his gun drawn and pointed at her. It happened so fast that Madison screamed. So did Lacy.

"What in the name of all that is holy are you doing down here?" he demanded, his gun still trained on her.

She clutched her heart as she cradled her baby. "I was trying not to disturb your sleep. She's teething," Madison explained, nodding toward her screaming baby. "And thanks to you I won't be getting the ice back in her mouth. It appears none of us will be sleeping tonight."

Ryan cursed and tossed his gun onto a bookshelf. "Great."

"Yeah, great," Madison agreed, tired, annoyed, and just about over the top with trying to get along with this man. "Another two minutes and her gums would have been soothed and she would have dropped off to sleep."

"I'm sorry, but I heard a noise, and it's my job to protect you. I was merely doing what I'm being paid to do."

Disgusted, she said, "Whatever," and tried again to get the ice into Lacy's mouth. But Lacy shrieked like a banshee and began to slap at her mother's hand and squirmed in such a way that Madison almost couldn't control her.

Ryan ran his hand down his face. "Look at her," he said sympathetically. "The poor little thing. Can't you do something?"

"Not now," she said, swallowing another angry accusation.

"Why is she doing all that?" Ryan asked, his voice steeped in concern, his blue eyes clouded with remorse.

"Because she's in pain," Madison said, watching him as he slowly made his way to the sofa. "Haven't you ever had a toothache?"

"Yes," Ryan said, vividly remembering his wisdom teeth. As quickly as that vision came so did another. He sprang from the couch and ran to Angus's bar. "We had a maid once, a young girl, about twenty-two," he said as he bent and opened the cabinet door. "Anyway, she lived in the house with us, and one night her kid did this very same thing."

He saw Madison eye him suspiciously as she continued to sooth her sobbing child, but otherwise she stayed silent. "I was about seventeen at the time and the kid scared the crap out of me, but Angus just came bustling into the kitchen, poured a shot of Scotch, dipped in his finger and rubbed it along the baby's gums. Ten minutes later she was sound asleep." He paused and grinned. "Part from the numbing of the alcohol, part from swallowing enough to relax her."

"Mr. Kelly, I'm not giving my child alcohol."

"I'm not asking you to," he said, pulling out the bottle and pouring a shot. "We'll be more careful than Angus was. We'll use it to numb her gums."

As he approached, she continued to give him her totally distrustful stare. In a way Ryan supposed he didn't blame her. Not only had he done nothing but argue with her since their arrival, but now he was trying to give her less-than-one-year-old child alcohol. No. He didn't blame her at all for being suspicious.

"Lacy's in luck," he said, turning up the charm by smiling as endearingly as he could. "This is some of Angus's best stuff. Twelve years old and expensive as a bride's trousseau. If nothing else, we'll know she's getting the best.''

He waited for Madison to answer; she said nothing. Luckily, Lacy hiked the tempo a notch and went from shrieking to screaming bloody murder.

"The effect of the ice is gone now.''

"I see that,'' Ryan said kindly, sat on the couch beside them and decided to take matters into his own hands. "Surely in all your research you've discovered that some of the old wives' tales, the things passed down from generation to generation, are the best cures.''

"I don't know of any mother who gave her child alcohol.''

"Angus's mother obviously did. And look how good he turned out. Isn't a better man this side of the Mississippi, or a healthier one, I might add,'' he said, slanting a glance at Madison, who, he could tell, was weakening. "Besides, we're not giving her alcohol, we're rubbing a little on her gums. That's all,'' Ryan said soothingly as he dipped his finger into the shot glass and casually slid it into Lacy's mouth. The shock of the intrusion silenced her. He slowly ran the drop of Scotch along her gums. She blinked her tear-filled eyes up at him.

"It hurts, doesn't it?'' he compassionately asked the baby, who simply gazed up at him, exhausted from the pain. "Well, we'll take care of this for you,'' he continued, dipping his finger again and again and running it along her gums. He rubbed the Scotch on her gums a few more times, then glanced at Madison for instructions.

"Why don't you get her a bottle?''

Ryan complied, then returned to the sofa, sitting beside Madison as she gave Lacy the bottle and cuddled the little girl to sleep against her bosom.

The only light in the entire cabin was the pale illumination that filtered in from the kitchen. The only sound, the soft suckling of a very sleepy child.

"When she's quiet like this it's hard to believe she can make as much noise as she does, isn't it?"

Though Ryan could tell she didn't want to, Madison smiled. "All babies can make a lot of noise. It's their sole way of getting what they want or telling you something's wrong."

"You've done a lot of research on this, haven't you?"

She glanced at him. He saw her debate whether to answer him, then give in to her good breeding. "Enough that when I had my own child I'd already had a subscription to *Parents* magazine."

Ryan drew a long breath and knew a better time wouldn't come along to apologize. "I'm sorry we keep arguing. We're on opposite poles of a disagreement neither one of us can win."

As the baby nestled closer, Madison held up her free hand. "Don't. Don't apologize again. The only thing *that* does is cloud the issue. We don't like each other. We don't get along. Let's just admit it and leave it at that."

"But we do get along. At least, we get along unless or until I compare you to my parents." He stopped, raked his fingers through his hair. "I don't know what happens to me, but every time we get into that argument, I feel like I'm nine years old again."

"And that's why you get upset," she said, casting a quick glance in his direction. "You're not angry with me. You're angry with your parents. You're taking it out on me, but you're really not angry with me. You don't know me well enough to be angry with me."

"That sounds like a fairly logical assumption. Don't tell me you read psychology books along with *Parents* magazine?"

"Of course."

"Then I guess I'm really in trouble."

Thinking he was teasing, she smiled again and shook her head, but when she looked at him his gaze was intense, serious. With one arm lying along the back of the sofa and the other across her lap, braced on the far side of her hip, he'd literally enveloped her and Lacy. Their faces were mere inches apart. She could see the rise and fall of his chest from his breathing.

This man who could be such an unprecedented pain in the backside, was the absolute epitome of sex appeal. Shirtless, with sleep tousled hair, wearing nothing but butter-soft silk pajama bottoms, he made her feel things she never thought she'd feel about a man. But more than that he was sincere, dependable, strong. In the same no-nonsense way that he'd saved her in her parking garage and unobtrusively taken care of them in this cabin for the past few days, he'd soothed her sobbing child. In the dim light of the silent room, his strength seemed to pulsate around them. It was that strength, she knew, that drew her. That strength she found sexier than his whiskery chin, his beautiful blue eyes, or even the hair-covered, well-muscled chest a few inches away from her hand.

He had leaned toward her sufficiently that Madison knew one signal from her and he'd kiss her. He wanted it. She wanted it. Aeons apart in personality, light years away in how they saw life, and, still, he wanted to kiss her and she wanted to let him.

She pulled away.

"Did you ever stop to think that maybe your comparing me to your parents is the best thing that could have happened for us?"

He cocked his head in question.

"If you weren't constantly accusing me of being like your parents I might actually like you. And being as attracted as we are, that would only mean trouble."

He ran a finger along her jawline. "I'm not exactly sure I'd agree with that half of your evaluation."

She felt her pulse jump and knew she was right. "I'm not a person who goes in for quick flings. If you think I am because I have Lacy, then you're not merely easily angered, you're stupid."

"I didn't say that."

She held up a hand to halt his indignant defense. "I'm just covering my bases, explaining that I'm not a person who goes in for quick flings. I'm also not the kind of person you'd marry. So we're right back where we started from." She raised her eyes until she caught his gaze. His blue eyes were earnest, questioning, and though Madison genuinely believed every word of what she was about to tell him, she also knew in some silent corner of her heart that it was already too late. All the common, ordinary things he'd done to make her comfortable in the past four days, coupled with his determined search for a tablet and pen, not to mention his ten minutes of gentleness with her daughter had her softening to him. Foolishly wishing that things could be different.

"We're nowhere. We're two people who wouldn't have met under normal circumstances, stuck with each other for a short period of time, who probably won't see each other again after this." The mere thought gave her a quick pang, but she silenced it. She was nothing, if not practical.

He continued to look at her, studying her with his solemn blue eyes. "I know you're right—"

"Of course I'm right," Madison interrupted, cutting him off before he could say more. She didn't want to argue or analyze this. It didn't make any sense, wasn't part of her plan any more than it was part of his. But more than that, she didn't want him to see that she found him handsome enough, steady enough, courageous enough, interesting enough that she'd risk a little bit of what she had to see if there was any future for them.

They both already knew he didn't feel the same. How could he imagine a future with a woman who lived a life he couldn't tolerate? She wouldn't express her feelings for him out loud and embarrass herself.

"She's sleeping soundly now," Madison said, indicating Lacy with a nod of her head. "I think it's time for me to get her to her crib."

"Let me carry her," Ryan volunteered quietly, still watching her, still assessing everything she said, every move she made.

She shook her head. "That will disturb her." She glanced over, smiling as pleasantly as she could. "You could give me a hand up, though."

He bounded to his feet and assisted her rising. When she would have pulled away, he pulled her back.

"This isn't over," he said, studying her with his steady blue eyes. "Not by a long shot."

She held his gaze. "I think it is. If you'll excuse me…"

Chapter Nine

Baby in her arms, Madison slowly made her way to the stairway. Ryan leaned back on the couch and, eyes narrowed as he watched Madison climb the steps, he smiled.

Even though Cal had said this before, it took hearing Madison say the words aloud before Ryan realized what he and Madison were doing wrong.

They were thinking happily ever after.

It was no wonder they couldn't get along. Instead of living in the moment, taking things one day, one hour, one minute at a time, they were trying to create a future.... And they had none. They argued and fussed and feuded and still came up empty-handed—when they could be accepting the situation for what it was, taking what they could get and being satisfied—maybe even happy—albeit for a few days.

It was so simple, yet it had been so hard to grasp.

Ryan drew a long breath and settled into the couch again. He didn't wonder about why he thought of her in terms of happily ever after. He wasn't in love—couldn't be in love, he'd only known her a few days. And he wasn't crazy. In fact, he wasn't anything. It was her. No man could look at her without thinking of marriage. She was a walking, talking, living, breathing advertisement for domesticity, simply by virtue of the products she produced. Baby clothes, strollers, high chairs, cribs. It was little wonder he saw a house with a white picket fence every time he looked at her. That was the image she'd cultivated. The image she promoted. It had nothing at all to do with reality. And certainly nothing to do with him.

So, the sole question left was how to handle this.

Ryan almost laughed. He knew exactly how he wanted to handle this. He wanted to sleep with her. He wanted to touch her, he wanted to kiss her, he wanted to do absolutely everything a normal man wanted to do with a woman to whom he was unbearably attracted. There was no question in his mind about how he planned to play this out. Come to think of it, he'd laid the groundwork when he'd almost promised to seduce her before letting her walk away.

Plus time was on his side, he thought, rising from the couch. They both had nothing but time. And according to Angus time cured everything.

The next morning Madison went downstairs to find not merely a delicious breakfast, but a cozy table. Dishes and silver had been placed appropriately, not haphazardly, and in the center, between the two place settings, was a small bouquet of wildflowers.

So that was it, then. He really did plan to seduce her.

"Sleep well?" he asked, sneaking up on her from behind and whispering the words in her ear.

She barely kept herself from jumping. "Yes, I slept very well," she said, feeling the warmth of his breath on her nape. Imagining his lips a mere millimeter from the tender skin sent a jagged bolt of heat through her.

This wasn't good, wasn't good at all, but addressing it

outright might cause another argument or give him an opening she might not be able to resist—though ignoring it might come across as permission of sorts.

Before she could decide, he surprised her by moving away. "Will Lacy sleep longer than normal since she was awake part of the night?"

Relieved but unnerved, Madison combed her fingers through her hair. "I hope."

"Good, that will give us time to chat."

She didn't want to chat. Well, actually, she didn't mind chatting. The whole problem was she knew what his chatting would lead up to. "I'm not exactly sure what we have to talk about."

"Why don't you tell me about your childhood?"

"That's not something I want to discuss."

"Why not?" he asked, then popped a fresh berry onto his tongue. Madison watched the small piece of fruit disappear into his mouth, and realized belatedly that she was staring at his lips.

"You told me I don't understand being poor," he said, cheerfully lobbing a scoop of scrambled eggs to her plate. "And maybe you're right. Maybe this is something I need to hear."

It almost sounded as if he was interested in understanding in order to help himself in his situation with his parents. To that end she couldn't refuse him. She sighed. "Well, being poor isn't as simple as not having money. It's more encompassing than that," she said, attempting to figure out how to explain this to him. "I remember once being at a dance when I was young. There was another girl there who had on the most perfect outfit, and everybody was making a fuss over it."

Since she'd chosen such an unlikely example, she peeked at Ryan to make sure he was listening, that she wasn't confusing him. He was right with her. Or at least he seemed to be.

"Anyway, I remember thinking I would dress like that. I would dress every bit as well as she did, if I had the money."

"So, being poor means you can't be the person you want to be."

He surprised her with his insight and she smiled. "Precisely."

"And having money means you are, right now, exactly the person you want to be."

She swallowed, realizing he'd sprung a trap and she'd walked right in. "Yes."

"That's very interesting," he said and took a bite of eggs. "If I'm interpreting you correctly, you're telling me that part of my parents' ambition could have been nothing more than a strong desire to be the people they wanted to be."

Madison's surprise that he was holding this discussion in such an objective way was edged out by the fact that his question was sincere. "Don't you know?" she asked incredulously.

He shook his head. "I told you, my parents rarely talked to me."

"Not even now?"

"Now, it's my choice, not theirs. Now, *I* don't have time in my life for them." He paused, considered, then said, "Actually, I guess the best way to put it is that our schedules don't coincide. Once in a great while I'll be able to get time off when they're scheduled to be at the villa. But not always. Even the few times they've arrived for visits with Angus, I've always been up to my ears in work."

"I think that's sad," Madison said, knowing she was moving them both into argument territory again, but not caring.

Ryan shrugged. "I guess it all depends on your vantage point. So, how'd you go to college?"

"Loans," Madison replied, impressed by how smoothly he'd changed the subject, but not ready to let it go. "You don't see, do you, that you're doing the same thing to your parents that they did to you?"

He looked at her. "Of course I see. But even though it seems the same, the situation is completely different. I'm not their parent, I'm not responsible for their health, safety and well-being like they were for mine. Want some bacon?"

"No, I do not want any bacon," she said, rising from her seat because he was making her mad. It wasn't because he wouldn't talk about this situation, but more because of how flippantly he discarded it. He didn't *want* to see any side but his own. Proof positive he hadn't given one iota. He was right. She was wrong. End of story.

"I think I'd better go upstairs and check on Lacy."

She got as far as the kitchen door before he slumped in his chair. *Damn it!* He'd done it again. He'd inadvertently led them to the one conversational topic they should avoid, and no matter how hard he'd tried, he couldn't get them back out again. He considered that that was because most of Madison's life seemed to revolve around work, but dismissed the idea. There were other things they could talk about. If it killed him, he would find them.

He would do much better next time.

But there wasn't a next time. Madison avoided him like the plague. Two days later the air was so thick with tension that Ryan was ready to say anything, do anything to get her to talk to him again. On the verge of begging, he stopped short when the sound of an approaching vehicle interrupted the absolute silence in Angus's cabin.

After grabbing his gun from the peg by the door, Ryan

positioned himself to look out the window. Curtain drawn, he peeked out, allowed himself a long sigh of relief, then dropped the curtain. "You can come out now," he called to Madison, and though he knew she heard him he wasn't sure she'd obey. He smiled and played his ace in the hole. "It's Jessica."

Baby balanced on her hip, she came bounding down the steps. "Jess!" she said, as the door opened and the tall, sophisticated DA entered the room. Apparently having taken a side trip from her regular daily duties, Jessica wore a cinnamon suit, white pumps and pearls.

"You look great!" Madison said, and Ryan heard the envy in her voice. Part of it he understood. Both he and Madison would kill to get back to their regular routines right now. The other part was a purely feminine thing women had about their appearance. An odd notion, Ryan thought. Given his choice between the two women, he'd take Madison in her T-shirt and jeans…. Then again, given a choice, actually given a choice, he'd take Madison over anyone. Suit, bathing suit or naked.

"You think I look great to you now," Jessica said, laughing. "Wait until you hear what I've got in the car."

"What have you got?" Madison asked excitedly as she handed her daughter to Jessica. The baby happily went to Jessica, an indication she'd done so a million times.

Ryan leaned against the kitchen doorjamb. After a week, he'd yet to as much as say hello to the kid. He felt awkward to realize Madison was this free with Lacy with Jessica, when she wouldn't even let him touch her.

"Not only did I bring several decks of cards and some board games," she said, her voice tempting and teasing, "but I also brought someone's portable PC." She bounced Lacy once. "I couldn't go to your office and get work," she said apologetically. "That would be a tip-off that you're not on vacation. But I did sneak into your house and get your computer.''

"Doesn't matter," Madison said, appearing so euphoric Ryan thought she'd dance for joy. "My work's all up here, anyway," she said, tapping her head.

"And I'll appreciate the cards," Ryan said, then turned away and went into the kitchen. "At least now I can play solitaire."

He walked away and Jessica faced Madison. "What's with him?"

Uncomfortable because she knew Ryan was a friend of Jessica's, Madison shrugged. "Beats me," she said, then she winced. "That's not true. I know why he's touchy. Every time we talk, we fight. Even when we tried to have a civil discussion the other day over breakfast, he insulted the hell out of me—unintentionally—and I decided that if we couldn't hold a civil conversation when both of us were on best behavior, it was much better for us not to talk, so we haven't."

"What?" Jessica said, then she laughed. "I can't believe that. First of all, Ryan's so damned bossy I can't believe you could get him to shut up for a few days. Second, Mary Sunshine," she said, tweaking Madison's cheek, "you're the one who never lets the sun set on her anger."

"Well, the sun has not only set and risen several times, but I'm just about certain it will set and rise several million more before I speak to him."

Jessica's face scrunched with confusion. "What in the hell do you two fight about?"

"It's ridiculous," Madison said, not wanting to get into it with Jessica. As she took Lacy from Jessica's arms, she changed the subject. "How long can you stay?"

"I was hoping to get some time with you to prep you for your testimony, which means I'll be here for a while. I might even stay for dinner."

"Well, that's one thing you're lucky on. I have to admit he is a terrific cook."

"Good. We'll get him to rustle up something while he's watching Lacy for us and you and I will run testimony."

Jessica stopped because Madison was shaking her head. "He can't watch Lacy."

"Why not?" Ryan asked from the doorway.

She lifted her chin. "Because."

"Because why? Because you don't want her to get to know me?"

"Because you haven't looked at her twice since we've been here. You've treated her as if she has the plague."

"*I* treated *her* as if she has the plague? You don't have any room to talk about treating someone as if they have the plague…"

"Whoa! Whoa!" Jessica intervened, physically stepping between them. "You have testimony to run," she said to Madison. "And you certainly are not the most congenial person on the face of the earth," she added, facing Ryan. "If Madison's been protective of Lacy, it might be because she doesn't understand that beneath that gruff exterior beats a heart of gold." She paused, faced Madison again. "That's true," she said kindly. "He'll be good to Lacy. Besides, it won't take us long."

Madison conceded the point with a nod and within minutes Lacy was in the kitchen, seated in her high chair with the tray piled with play things while Madison and Jessica took up residence on the sun porch and began going over her testimony.

Ryan peered in the cupboards, trying to decide what to cook for dinner. He told himself he wanted to impress Jessica, but the truth was he wanted to prove to Madison that he could not only take good care of her daughter but he could make a fantastic dinner while he did so.

* * *

"I know you were on your best behavior tonight."

Jessica's car taillights hadn't even disappeared before Madison rounded on Ryan. She didn't mean to complain to Jessica, but eventually Jessica got her to pour her heart out about how Ryan did nothing but criticize her. Though Jessica had laughed and genuinely seemed to understand, because she knew Ryan had a tendency to be bossy and overbearing, Madison felt like an absolute fool when Ryan behaved nothing like the ill-tempered maniac Madison had described.

"Would it have been more appropriate for me to apologize?"

About to turn away, Madison stopped short. "What are you talking about?"

"All I was trying to do the other morning was prove to you that on some level or another we could get along." He paused, shrugged. "That conversation didn't work. But I don't put a whole hell of a lot of stock in words, anyway. This afternoon I realized I could set things right better with actions rather than words. So I watched your child, fixed a great dinner and let you have a little quality time with your friend." He stopped and caught her gaze. "But even that didn't please you."

His answer made her feel small and churlish. She raked her fingers through her hair. "It's not that what you did today didn't please me. I suppose the best way to explain it is that I don't trust it when you do something nice for me. I keep waiting for the other shoe to fall."

Smiling self-deprecatingly, he said, "There are no other shoes. I'm trying to get along with you. I *want* to get along with you."

As he said the words, he shoved his hands in his pockets as if he needed to do that to keep from touching her. The gesture was as endearing as it was erotic. She pulled her fingers through her hair again. "Okay, I know this isn't your fault any more than it's mine. I know we have some sort of strange chemistry. I'm not pointing a finger at you or making you feel like you're to blame.''

''That's good to hear.''

''Well, I'd be less than honest if I didn't admit it.''

He smiled. ''And perfect Madison Delaney is nothing if not honest.''

She smiled. ''It's not a crime.''

''No, it's not,'' he agreed. ''And I would know because I'm a policeman.''

''Yes, you would. From what Jessica tells me you're a very good policeman, too.''

''I am,'' he agreed easily. ''Just like you're very good at figuring out what makes babies tick.''

''Why, Sheriff Kelly, if I didn't know better I'd think that was a compliment.''

''You deserve a great deal of credit for the things you do. I've seen how well adjusted your child is, how happy. I know that all those contraptions she plays with, the things you invented, have a great deal to do with how contented she is. It doesn't take a genius to figure out that if Lacy's this happy, then so are the ten million other kids who play with your toys. You didn't get rich because you were lucky, Madison, you got rich because you're smart.''

It wasn't what he said, but how he said it that caused her to see he meant it. Until that moment, Madison hadn't realized how much his approval meant to her. Not that he appreciated what she did, but that he recognized that what she did had value beyond providing money and a certain amount of fame.

Unexpectedly touched, she swallowed. Maybe he wasn't so bad after all. ''Thanks.''

''You're welcome,'' he said, then took her bicep and directed her to the wooden plank steps of the porch. ''Care to sit out on the swing and have a beer with me?'' he asked, then faced her again. "Lacy's sound asleep and the moon is full and perfect for watching. God knows, there's not too much else to do."

She was tempted, sorely tempted to just say yes. The moon was full, a bright silver ball that sprinkled shimmering light to the leaves of the trees. The warm night air misted around them. And she hadn't had a beer in the past five years. Hadn't rested, relaxed in the last ten. Somehow the beer and the rest seemed long overdue. With every intention of agreeing, she glanced up into Ryan's eyes, and what she saw there stopped any words from forming on her tongue.

For every bit as quickly as one sort of tension had evaporated, another took its place. With the backdrop of the thick forest, and the moonlight washing over him, Ryan Kelly was about as handsome as a man could get. The combination of his perfectly formed features, the high cheekbones, cleft chin and his brilliant blue eyes with their steady gaze sent her heart thumping.

And that's what always got them into trouble. They were, right now, exactly where they always were when they let their guards down and ended up fighting.

Ryan thought they were exactly where they were supposed to be. Lips about a half inch apart, palms and fingers itching to touch and explore, bodies tingling with anticipation....

Though the temptation was strong to seize the moment and kiss her, he suddenly realized it was the wrong thing to do. He'd become predictable in the way that he wanted her, and that was very easy for her to fight or ignore. He didn't want her to fight him anymore. And he sure as hell didn't want her ignoring him, either.

Maybe it was time to switch tactics.

He looked at her pink lips, then up into her amber eyes. She wouldn't fight him for the first few minutes. Her lips would be soft and pliant. She would let him slide his palm along her cheek, down her nape, maybe even across a need-swollen breast. It was tempting.

But he also knew she'd freeze. At some point, she'd remember their arguments and disagreements, she'd pull away, and they'd be right back where they started from, arguing and fighting, ignoring and compromising, until they got to this point again. And he didn't want to be here anymore. He wanted to go farther, much farther.

Pure discipline overwhelmed impulse and he stepped away from her. "You go ahead to bed," he said, glancing around as if looking for something important. "I think I'll wait up a bit—check the woods—make sure Jessica wasn't followed."

"Okay," she said, sounding relieved.

But mingled with that relief he heard confusion. She had expected him to kiss her and didn't have a clue why he hadn't.

She turned and jogged up the plank porch steps, and Ryan smiled.

Finally he had the upper hand.

Chapter Ten

After breakfast Madison took Lacy into the sunroom where she played quietly while Madison worked on her computer. After a few minutes of pounding away on the keyboard, she heard a sound and looked up to see Ryan had poked his head into the sunroom. He announced that he was going to take a trip around the grounds to be sure no one was anywhere near them, and though Madison thought that odd—as odd as him waiting up until all hours the night before to be sure no one had followed Jessica—she didn't question Ryan. She merely nodded her acknowledgment of the fact that he was leaving and went back to work.

When he returned two hours later, Lacy was in bed and Madison had moved her computer to a game table in the main room. Ryan put his Stetson on a peg by the door, then approached her. "What are you working on?" he asked considerately.

"Nothing important," Madison replied, stretching to get the kinks out of her back. "I'm just gathering ideas."

"Then maybe you wouldn't mind taking a break from that to play a little Monopoly."

She scowled. "Not Monopoly. How about Battle Ship?"

"Ah, a strategist."

"Precisely," she said, and smiled with feline satisfaction. "By the time I was twelve, I could beat anyone."

"Well, we'll see about that," Ryan said, grabbing the Battle Ship box from the stack of goodies Jessica had provided.

Companionably both assembled their game pieces. Ryan won the coin toss and took the first move. Unfortunately the game only lasted ten minutes. Madison correctly anticipated how he would position his ships, and she literally annihilated him.

Frustrated, he raked his fingers through his already unruly hair. "Rematch," he said quietly, and Madison happily complied. In fact, she happily complied four times.

"How do you do that?" he growled, as he was pulling his game pieces off after the fifth game.

She shrugged. "It isn't long before I figure out how a person thinks. The first game I guessed your typical strategy based on your personality type. The second game I knew you'd go as far away from your strategy as possible. From there it was a matter of finding your first ship. Once I found your first ship I could pretty much figure out where you'd put all the others."

"You should be in law enforcement."

"Fat chance," Madison replied pleasantly. "I'd much rather use my gifts to anticipate needs than figure out problems."

Ryan considered that. In a nutshell that was her personality. And it was another one of those things that appealed to him about her. The way she solved problems before they became problems was like a breath of fresh air—particularly to someone who put in his eight-hour workday cleaning up other people's messes.

"I guess you do," he agreed, realizing he'd finally stumbled into pay dirt. This could be the magic morning that changed their relationship from adversarial to companionable. If they played games long enough, they could potentially discover enough good things about each other to let their guards down. And once they let their guards down...

As if on cue, Lacy began to wail.

"Must be lunchtime," Madison said as she rose from her seat and started running to the stairway.

Ryan resisted the urge to slap the table. That kid had lousy timing. He glanced at his watch and, with a gasp, realized Lacy's timing had been much better than he'd imagined. "Holy cow, it's after one."

"She's probably starved," Madison said from the steps. "I'll start lunch."

While he quickly prepared their meal, Ryan decided that Lacy's interruption didn't need to ruin everything. He'd go back to his original strategy. When Madison expected him to make a move, make a pass or screw things up, he'd retreat. Confuse her. And not only would he eventually muddle her thinking to the point that she'd forget she didn't like him, but leaving every once in a while also seemed to keep them from fighting.

Who said he wasn't a strategist?

When Madison entered the kitchen, he turned and smiled. "You know," he said, edging toward the door, "I don't think it would hurt for me to take one more look around. You know, check things out." He pulled open the back door and slipped outside.

Madison watched him leave with a mixture of curiosity and frustration. Every time they seemed to come to a sort of understanding, a place where they could actually converse, he left. Irritated, she sat down to feed her child and realized he had her so perplexed, she wasn't paying attention to Lacy. She put Ryan Kelly and his strange moods out of her mind and fed her child.

By the time Ryan came back, Lacy was in napping again and Madison was back at her computer. She and Lacy had eaten their lunch, walked around the cabin and played in the sunroom. Through their entire walk, Madison had expected to find Ryan around the next tree but they never ran into him. The fresh air and exercise had tired Lacy and she easily, happily went down for her nap. And now, when Madison was ready to break from her computer again, in the door walked Ryan Kelly.

It was almost as if he'd read her mind.

"Ready for a rematch, or would you like to try your luck at something else?"

"Actually," Madison said slowly, "I'm not the kind of person who can sit all day, and after three hours of board games this morning and another hour at the computer now, I've had enough."

"You want to go for a walk?"

She shook her head. He had a strange, confident air about him. She guessed that was because he was glad they hadn't argued yet today. But it was more than that. He had a cat-that-swallowed-the-canary gleam in his eyes. And she pretty much figured she knew the cure for that. "I already took Lacy for a walk. Besides, I want to do something more productive than walking," she said and strolled past him. "I could straighten up one of the rooms, but the only thing I haven't cleaned is the front porch."

Though he hadn't moved, Ryan's gaze followed her. "Angus isn't going to recognize this place, as it is. If you clean the front porch he'll think he's at the wrong cabin."

"I don't think we need to worry about that," Madison said on her way to the kitchen. "Since I'm going to sweep the porch, not rebuild it."

Ryan watched her walk away and nearly cackled with glee. He had her so confused she was telling him what she was going to do, not keeping her every move a secret. This was a definite step in the right direction. When she returned with two brooms instead of one, he only squinted at her.

"Come on," she said, handing him a broom. "A little physical activity will be good for you, too."

Ryan had had all the physical activity he needed today. He'd used his long walks not merely to get out of the cabin, but also to get his body moving in order to forget how much he wanted this woman. He glanced at the broom, then at Madison. In a T-shirt and jeans, her yellow hair pulled into a bouncy knot of curls at the top of her head, and a small smile bowing her full pink lips, she looked about as delectable as a woman could look. Soft and feminine, yet devilishly spirited. He felt his muscles tighten. Maybe a little more physical activity wouldn't hurt?

He took the broom.

Madison walked to the far right corner of the porch, so Ryan started working in the far left. Scowling, he angled the broom to get the cobwebs from the corner and wondered what it was about this woman that tempted him so much that he did stupid things like bring flowers for the breakfast table, take long walks to make her miss him and clean the porch to get his mind off begging her to sleep with him. Any other woman he could forget in fifteen minutes, but this one lived in his thoughts, invaded his dreams and didn't want him.

Not that he blamed her. Before he'd realized he didn't need to think in terms of happily ever after with Madison, he had made it very clear he didn't like her life. She had more money than she needed and still she worked. That decision didn't interfere with her child. No, she adored and cared for Lacy wonderfully, but in a sense that ensured that she didn't have time for a relationship.

In fact, he'd come to realize that was probably why she hadn't married Lacy's father.

"Excuse me," Madison said, walking over to Ryan's half of the porch. "What did you say about Lacy's father?"

Embarrassed, Ryan glanced up. "I didn't say anything about Lacy's father."

"Yes, you did. You mumbled the whole time you were swiping cobwebs from the wall, and I didn't understand a word of it until you said Lacy's father."

"I was just thinking," Ryan said, and put his broom to the plank floor, tremendously relieved she hadn't heard anything but his last few mumbles. "It's not important."

"If you have a question about Lacy's father," Madison said stubbornly, "any question, I'll be happy to answer it."

Right at that moment Ryan realized he wanted to know. He really wanted to know. Though it hadn't seemed important because of all the other things between them, right now it suddenly ranked right up there with mysteries of the universe.... And she seemed like she wouldn't mind telling him.

"I've considered explaining before, because I thought it might ease some of the tension between us for me to explain."

He'd never thought of that, but she might be right. Her confession might ease some of their "other" tension. It might make her comfortable enough with him that they could go to the next level sexually. He stopped his broom. "So, what happened?"

She drew a long breath. "Bluntly, I simply didn't love him." She picked up her broom and started to sweep again. "I believed I did, but when I got pregnant and started seeing him as a father, I realized he didn't have what it took to be a father." She paused, made two more swipes with her broom. "But what was worse," she said, as if she'd decided to reveal a confidence she'd not revealed before, "was that he didn't seem to want to *try* to be a father. He wanted Lacy to have nannies twenty-four hours a day, and I couldn't do that."

Her heartfelt confession had the effect of a slap across the side of the head and gave Ryan a horrible case of guilt. This was a serious, noble woman he was attempting to seduce. A woman who didn't take sex or children or anything lightly. He felt like hell.

Busying himself with cobwebs in the corner, he said, "It almost seems like it embarrasses you to tell me that."

"Well, Lacy does have a nanny and three rotating baby-sitters. So, I almost sound hypocritical. But I'm not. Her nanny works with us during the day and when we travel. The sitters handle night detail when I need to go out. But I'm with her every day between four and seven. I also spend time every morning with her, since we're early risers. So, yes, she is frequently in the care of another person, but I also spend a great deal of time with her."

Ryan studied her. "Why are you defensive?"

"Because I always feel like I'm in the middle of a battle. Proving to people like you that I spend enough time with her, even as I fight my staff to hold on to the private time I do get. Most executives don't leave at four o'clock, you know."

"Boy, do I know," Ryan said, and right then and there decided his last battleship had been blown out of the water. He couldn't seduce a woman like this. If he did, he would hate himself. He'd *deserve* to hate himself. Unless he could take this woman for happily ever after, then he had no business touching her. "If it's any consolation I admire you for sticking by your guns. I wish my mother had felt the way you do about making sure she had some time with me."

"How do you know your mother didn't feel that way? Better yet, how do you know your *parents* didn't feel that way? How do you know they weren't forced into working that many hours?''

Ryan went back to sweeping. "My parents were not *forced* into working. We had plenty of money. There was no 'need' for my parents to work the way they did. Besides, my mother didn't have a job. She was a social butterfly who spent all her time working for charities." He stopped, stared at her until he caught her gaze, and smiled. He wasn't going to fight again. He really wasn't. His past wasn't her problem. In fact, his past hadn't even been a problem for him until he met her and she made him remember things he'd dealt with many, many years ago.

When he said his next words he knew they were the absolute truth, the bottom line, so to speak, to his life. ''And all that's history. Gone. Finished. I'm not bitter or stupidly resentful. I simply refuse to make the same mistakes myself.''

When they first started this conversation, Madison couldn't help but see a small boy hungry for his parents' love, affection and attention, and her heart went out to him. But as they talked, she continued to watch him, studied his expressions, considered the tone and finality of his words and knew he didn't hold a grudge. He wasn't angry. He really was adjusted. Now that he'd gotten past the confusion of being attracted to someone whose lifestyle resembled his parents', he showed his true colors. He had been hurt, but it didn't ruin his life.

Given that she'd grown up poor and struggled to earn her own way without having money as her only goal, Madison had a great deal of respect for anybody who had a difficult childhood and still managed to grow up a balanced human being. But Ryan Kelly was more than a well-balanced human being. He'd created exactly the life that he wanted, and he guarded it jealously. He enjoyed his life, loved and respected Angus and found a rewarding, challenging place for himself in the community. He was, in a word, content.

It was another thing to like about him. There was no pretense or artifice. He was who he was. And she found that absolutely irresistible—which was probably why she was falling in love with him. He knew what he wanted. Without qualm or apology he knew what he wanted and he wouldn't settle for anything less.

"I still have a little trouble understanding why you work," Ryan said softly, reminding Madison that on a lot of levels *she* was something he wanted, but her life didn't fit into his plans. And she couldn't change herself to fit his plans. Now that they were talking seriously, openly, she might as well explain this, too.

"I have a gift, Ryan." She paused and smiled. "You can't have a gift and ignore it. I happen to be good with kids, not merely in a motherly way, but in that strategic way that combines anticipation with art. I see what they want, what they like, what they need, and somehow blend them all together to make life more fun for them as I make life safer and easier. I can't ignore that."

"No, I suppose you can't."

"Like I can't ignore my charities because I know that's another tangible way I can make a difference."

"I know you probably won't believe this, but I admire the way you make a difference."

The cobwebs were now gone. The logs of the front wall had been brushed clean. The floor was swept. They met in the middle of the wood plank porch, each with a new respect for the other.

She smiled, proud of the little boy in him who had suffered tremendous pain but refused to let that ruin his life. He'd come through it a strong, smart, determined man. The kind of man she could admire, respect and even love.

He smiled, knowing her motivations went beyond money

and even duty to something honorable and good. Her work had value. What she did would last forever. True, she probably wouldn't make the perfect wife. But she was a terrific mother and a humanitarian. The kind of person he could admire, respect and in some way—that combined admiration, respect and genuine affection—love.

Without further consideration or deliberation, Ryan put his index finger under her chin, tipped it up and bent to brush a light kiss across her lips. There was none of the passion and fire of the first kiss, but Madison knew this kiss was a hundred times more dangerous. A genuine affection had begun to grow between them, and that was more potent than lust.

Chapter Eleven

Ryan pulled away. The feelings churning through him were clearly reflected in Madison's stormy eyes. A gentle kiss had accomplished all the things his passionate kisses couldn't. Right now, right at this very minute, she wanted him. He'd gotten exactly what he'd been trying for. Only now he couldn't take advantage of it.

"I think I'll go take a walk around the grounds again," he said softly, then set his broom against the wall and started down the steps. *Damn her, anyway! Why did she have to be so good and pure and decent?*

Touching her fingertips to her lips, Madison watched him walk away. She didn't feel guilty about her work anymore, and it wasn't a stumbling block. An odd sensation fluttered through her. It felt very much like the realization that they were on the verge of something good—something permanent—even though Ryan obviously didn't see it that way. She was different from his parents. He seemed to understand that now. As far as she was concerned, the other problems they had could be handled or worked out, and her assignment over the next week would be to make him see that.

She turned to go into the cabin, and the phone began to ring. Not wanting to wake Lacy, she ran to answer it.

"I didn't think Ryan would let you answer the phone," Jessica said with a laugh when Madison said hello.

"He's out," she said, then peered through the open doorway to see that he had already gone so far she'd never be able to call him back. "Why? Did you need him?"

"No, I'm only calling to check up on the two of you. Things between you seemed better when I left last night."

Taking a seat, Madison said. "Last night when you left, I wanted to strangle him."

"Don't scare me, Madison."

"It's true," Madison said, then she laughed. "Then this morning we played board games and this afternoon we had a good discussion, and things changed for the better—I think," she amended, wondering if trying to make him see they could have a permanent relationship was a change for the better or the advent of more stormy weather. "My guess is you no longer have to worry that we're going to kill each other."

"That's always good for a district attorney to hear about a star witness and her favorite sheriff."

At Jessica's distraught tone, Madison laughed. "Let me put it to you this way, we may not be getting along perfectly fine yet, but there's no reason for you to be upset about the fact that we fight."

"I need you at a trial and him as an employee—I think I have plenty of reason."

Defeated, Madison sighed and gave up. "Jess, Ryan and I fight because we like each other."

"Oh, that makes sense."

"It does when you realize that we're attracted to each other but can't do anything about it."

"You're consenting adults who can do what they want."

"Not really."

Jessica took a short pause, and Madison wasn't surprised that her voice was cautious when she asked, "Why not?"

"Do you know much about his past?"

"I know everything about his past. Why?"

"Then you should have realized that he doesn't want to marry someone who's dedicated to her career, and I'm not going to marry someone who would ask me to leave everything I've built over the past ten years. So we're sort of at an impasse."

Madison heard Jessica's indrawn breath. "You've talked about *marriage?*"

"It's the strangest thing between us. We passed all the usual getting-to-know-someone rituals and fell right into that conversation...mostly, I think, because he sees too much of his parents' life in mine."

"And he's right."

Suddenly angry, Madison stiffened. "How do you know he's right? How does *he* know he's right? I'm nothing like his parents."

"That's not the issue," Jessica replied with unparalleled authority. "The issue is your lifestyle. If you're thinking that he's jumping to inaccurate conclusions, then you don't understand what's happening here. Do you realize that his parents basically gave him up at age sixteen?"

"He said Angus took him in at age sixteen, but it sounded like he had his parents' support."

"Yes and no. He was a problem child, and they gave up on him. Angus volunteered to keep him, and they were happy that he did. But they would have let Ryan try to find his own way in life. At age sixteen, they would have let him go out into the world...on his own. When he actually tells the story in full detail, it's very easy to see his parents didn't want him.''

"Are you telling me they abandoned him?"

"In a sense, yes," Jessica said. "But more than that, Madison, to recover from that hurt, Ryan rationalized that his parents' lifestyle didn't support having a child. So when he began to recover, he didn't blame himself or even his parents. He blamed their *lifestyle*. I think that's what made it easy for him to get over the hump of knowing his parents didn't want him.''

"Makes sense," Madison mumbled, leaning back in her chair.

"I don't think you understand what I'm telling you. When Ryan chooses to have a relationship, it will have to be one that provides him with stability and comfort. He needs a wife, a house and a white picket fence."

"Sort of the opposite from me."

"Unfortunately."

"So in a sense we're backward."

"It's more than that, Madison," Jessica said, sighing. "When Ryan walked away from his parents, he walked away from a guaranteed position with any one of their companies. He walked away from millions of dollars. He walked away from things the rest of us dream about. And he never looked back."

She paused, and Madison licked her dry lips. She knew what was coming next.

"Madison, he didn't work that hard to separate himself from that kind of life to take it back by marrying someone who not only has the same lifestyle his parents had, but who has more money than they do.

"You would do very well to remember all that," Jessica added candidly, "since I know you would never break down your companies to become a stay-at-home wife. You wouldn't do that to your employees anymore than you'd do that to your charities.''

"You're telling me there's absolutely no way he'd ever accept my life. That he wouldn't even try.''

''He doesn't have to try it to know it doesn't work for him. He's a smart man, Madison.''

"Yeah, well, I'm a pretty smart lady, Jessica. And I think you're both wrong.''

"Are you willing to risk Ryan's heart to prove it?''

"Now you're being dramatic.''

"No, you're closing your eyes to the obvious. Because that's what's at stake here. You push him too hard, too far, too fast, you're going to break his heart.''

Madison was awakened by a loud clap of thunder. Sliding out of bed, she craned her neck to see into Lacy's crib and realized that though she wasn't able to sleep through this storm, her baby was. Sighing, she decided a glass of water wouldn't hurt and walked out of the room. She knew that the reason Lacy could sleep—and she couldn't—was that Lacy wasn't worried about Ryan Kelly.

As she thought his name she met him in the hall. With his sleep-tousled hair and wearing only his pajama bottoms he looked about as sexy as a man could look. And she longed to simply step into his arms, but she couldn't.

Jessica wasn't the sort to be melodramatic, and, in fact, the things she said actually explained most of Ryan's behavior. Still, in the back of her mind Madison couldn't help but believe that when two people loved each other, silly problems like money and lifestyle were things that could be worked out.

"Storm wake you?'' Ryan whispered, walking down the hall toward her as she stepped out of her room.

Closing her bedroom door, she nodded.

"Want some cocoa?''

"That would be great, thank you."

He motioned for her to precede him down the stairs. They went to the kitchen, and while he warmed the milk on the stove, Madison rummaged until she found the cocoa.

"Go ahead into the main room," he instructed, pouring the warm milk into two mugs. "I'll be in in a minute."

Thunder rolled again. Flashes of lightning illuminated the main room. Wind rattled the windows.

"I'm surprised Lacy is sleeping through this," Ryan said, bringing the cocoa into the main room. He began to set the cups on the low table in front of the sofa, and Madison edged two coasters toward him. He glanced at her, glanced at the coasters and did what he knew she wanted him to do. But when he eased back on the couch, he said, "This is a cabin, Madison. Cup rings and cobwebs are part of the experience. I understood your wanting to clean up when we first came since we'd be 'living' here for two weeks. But there's no reason to be a fanatic about it."

Hearing what he was telling her, Madison laughed. "I suppose not," she agreed, then nodded toward his cocoa. "If you want to take your cup off the coaster, I'll understand."

He chuckled and shook his head. The cabin became quiet again, except for the intermittent claps of thunder and the rattle of the wind. It was a peaceful time, and Madison had the sense that they'd stolen these few minutes. Hundreds of questions she had about Ryan came tumbling to mind, and try as she might she couldn't stop herself from seeking answers.

The wind rattled the windows, lightning lit the large room. She looked over at him. "Ryan, Jessica told me today that you gave up a position with your father's company."

"I don't think I'd make much of a banker."

She considered his temperament, his disposition, the way

he always seemed to want to be outside and she smiled. "No, I guess not," she agreed. "But she also told me that you gave up millions of dollars because you refused the job."

"I'm going to have to have a long talk with Jessica."

"Don't be angry with her," Madison said. "She's concerned about you and told me things to help me understand you."

He peeked at her over the rim of his cup. "And why would you need to understand me?"

"You know we like each other. We both know we leaped right from getting introduced to seeing each other as a potential marriage partner."

Since he'd had the same conversation with Cal, Ryan didn't argue. Thunder seemed to roll over the cabin roof. Rain drummed on the windows. From the look on Madison's face, Ryan could tell she was searching for a way to make a point. He sat back, said nothing and waited.

"I'm worth a great deal of money, too."

Smiling into his cup, Ryan said, "Is that a fact?"

"Don't tease me," she said and rose to begin to pace. "This isn't easy for me."

He set his cup down on the table. "Then just say what you have to say, Madison, I'm not going to bite your head off."

"Okay," she said, turning to face him. "Because I have so much money, I feel a *responsibility* to not only share my wealth but also to make a *personal* commitment to certain charities, particularly children's charities."

"I know what that means, Madison. It means that you're not the kind of person to write a check and forget about it. You don't merely support your charities financially, you help them out by attending the balls, benefits and banquets." He paused, caught her gaze. "You lend your name, you give your time."

"Exactly," she said, and fell to the sofa again, relieved that he really did seem to understand.

"If you're telling me that getting involved with you would mean that I would have to accompany you to all those balls and banquets and benefits, I already figured that out." Not quite sure of the point she was trying to make, Ryan rose and walked to the window. He itched to touch her. Though she had a certain air of perfection about her, she was very touchable, very approachable, very real. And right at this moment, with her hair slightly sleep tousled and her body cozily warm from her cocoa and the covers, he knew exactly what her skin would feel like under his palm. He knew a lot of things about her instinctively and from watching her over the past week. He knew she was open, generous, kind. She was absolutely everything he would have wanted in a woman if and when he decided to settle down. But she was also committed elsewhere. And he couldn't have half a relationship...half a wife.

"Would it be so bad to have to accompany me to a few charity events?"

So they were bargaining, negotiating, he thought and turned from the window to face her. If she really wanted all the cards on the table, he'd put them there. "It might not be all that bad," he said, catching her gaze and holding it. "But it would be hypocritical. I couldn't do to a child what my parents did to me. I couldn't spend every night, or every weekend, or even every other weekend on other people's kids while my own sat at home wondering where I was."

"Most of the time Lacy's asleep when I leave. She doesn't sit at home wondering where I am."

"Maybe not now and maybe not when she's six, but when she's ten she'll wonder and then she'll rebel." Looking at Madison, seeing the expression of confusion on her face, Ryan knew she didn't quite grasp what he was telling her yet. Though he did now understand the point of her conversation. She was such an optimist that she always believed things would work out for the best. From experience, Ryan knew they wouldn't. "Maybe, Madison, I'm not the one who has to reconsider his life choices here. Maybe you're the one who needs to examine the way you're doing things and change now before it's too late."

He couldn't stay in this dim room, with her acquiescent and pleading, and not touch her. He set his cup on the table. "I'll see you in the morning," he said, then headed for the stairs. Before he set his foot on the bottom step, however, he added, "With all your money, and all your creativity, I'm surprised you haven't solved this problem before now. Not for me, not for a man, but for Lacy." He waited until he caught her gaze. "Think about it."

Chapter Twelve

While Ryan strolled the grounds, "checking the perimeter" as he always called it, Madison decided to make dinner. She needed something to occupy her mind. She couldn't work. She felt guilty ever since Ryan made his comments about reconsidering her life choices—not because she left her baby with a nanny now, but because of what might happen to Lacy in the future.

He was right. Damn him. As a baby, Lacy didn't require the time and attention an older child needed. But an older child did need more attention, a different kind of affection and much, much more time—time she hadn't budgeted into her schedule because Lacy didn't need it.

In other words, Ryan Kelly had her feeling guilty for things that hadn't even happened yet, for decisions she hadn't made, since she hadn't needed to make them.

All right, she thought, scanning the cupboard for something to make that didn't involve beans, eggs or lunch meat. She spied two cans of tomato sauce and grabbed them. *So he was right?* Given Lacy's age, what did it matter that one small-town sheriff knew from firsthand experience that quality-time parenting didn't work for older kids? All that really meant was that her life would have to change in the future.

Finding some peppers, oregano and a frozen pork chop, she set about to make spaghetti sauce, knowing in her heart that one didn't decide to change their life in the future. The future started today. Bit by bit, little by little, she had to get more free time for Lacy.

Maybe that wasn't right either. Maybe the operative word was *free*. Maybe she didn't need "free" time. Maybe what she needed was a way to spend *more* time with Lacy. The question was how?

One answer came quickly and easily. With as influential as she was with many of her favorite charities, she should be able to talk them into holding events which she and Lacy could attend together. Rather than host a charity ball on Saturday evening, they could have a circus on Saturday afternoon. Of course that would mean that she could no longer *hide* Lacy. She couldn't protect her from tabloids or curiosity seekers or even the questions and rumors about her father…

Madison paused, considered that. She didn't get the usual lump of fear in the pit of her stomach when she contemplated bringing Lacy out in public. It could be because the past ten days of having Lacy around a man who was a relative stranger had eased some of her anxiety. It could be because Lacy was older now and was ready to be exposed to her mother's life. She shrugged, reached for the oregano. Whatever the reason, introducing Lacy to the world no longer seemed like such a frightening thing. In fact, she found it exciting.

So, one segment of this dilemma was handled. If a charity wanted her to attend an event, they'd simply have to make it something she could attend with Lacy.

Buoyed with the excitement of this new development in her life, Madison happily put together her two-hour spaghetti sauce. It had been a long time since she cooked, she realized, humming happily as she pinched her spices and added the lone onion she found in a drawer....

And that was another thing she knew she needed to correct. She liked to cook. She wanted to cook. She *would* cook. Actually, cooking was only a part of what she felt she wanted right now. What she really wanted, wanted more than anything else, was to make a home.

Gasping, she stopped. That was it. That was what had been bugging her for the past day. She wanted to make a home. Lacy needed a home.

Ryan needed a home.

She wanted to make a home.

Laughter bubbled in her throat. Suddenly, it all seemed too easy.

"I've been thinking."

Ryan looked up from his reading to find Madison standing in front of him. She'd commandeered the kitchen, and the scents that filled the air had his mouth watering every bit as much as the sight of her standing before him.

"Is it safe to ask what you were thinking about?"

She burst into a bubbly giggle. The sound was so foreign Ryan concentrated on listening to the music of her voice, enjoying her laugh, knowing he didn't hear it often enough. Madison had been so serious, so focused, that he wondered if she ever let go. That notion gave him the strangest feeling, sort of like a flutter in his chest. He liked her light, lilting laugh enough that he wanted to laugh with her. He wanted to make her laugh again. And that was a dangerous, dangerous thought for a man who knew they didn't have very many more tomorrows. Ideas like that might make him want to borrow tomorrows, to experiment with a future.

And given their situation that wouldn't be wise. In the real world she'd be busy, unavailable and distant. A future for them simply wasn't possible. It would never work, and he wasn't about to fool himself with wishful thinking.

"Let's have dinner and I'll explain."

Cautious, Ryan rose from his seat and followed her into the kitchen. Lacy was already seated in her green, blue and yellow Kidtastic high chair, patting the tray with her chubby little hands. Ryan smiled at the baby, but he didn't say anything, and he definitely didn't even *think* of touching her, not even after having cared for her for an entire afternoon. Madison was too protective, and he was too awkward. The last thing Ryan wanted to do was risk inadvertently making this kid cry. Besides, he knew Madison kept this child a well-guarded secret. A person didn't go to the lengths that Madison had gone to, to let their secret daughter get too friendly with a policeman who'd be disappearing from their life in another couple of days. It was a significant victory that she'd trusted him enough to let him watch Lacy while she ran testimony with Jessica.

"Why don't you entertain Lacy for a minute while I strain this spaghetti?"

Her question caught him so much by surprise that Ryan stared at her back.

"What do you mean, *entertain her?*" he asked, stupefied.

Madison glanced at him over her shoulder and smiled. "Just talk to her."

Ryan looked at the semitoothless child, grinning up at him from her perch in her plastic high chair. Clearing his throat, he sat at the head of the table close to her chair. He tapped his fingers on her tray and smiled. "Hello, Lacy."

She grinned at him.

"You certainly are a cute little thing."

Lacy agreed wholeheartedly by laughing and slapping her hands on her tray.

"And noisy."

Lacy conceded that point with a high-pitched sound that was somewhere between a laugh and a squeal.

"Okay," Madison announced, bringing a bowl of pasta to the table. "Dinner's ready."

"Great, I'm starved," Ryan said, turning to face the table. "And sick of my own cooking. If I'd known you wanted to cook, I would have let you start days ago."

"I didn't know days ago that I wanted to cook."

Again, it wasn't the kind of answer he was expecting. In the middle of dishing out some spaghetti onto his plate, he stopped. "But you do this like a professional."

"Well, I've always been very good at anything domestic. Because my mother worked, I took over most of the household responsibilities. It's how I got to be good with kids and how I learned to cook."

"Ah," Ryan said, putting together puzzle pieces in his head. "That certainly makes sense."

"And it also explains how I could exploit my expertise, even though I've had this driving need to stay out of the house by having a career."

"Yes it does," Ryan agreed, watching her. What she'd just told him was a confession of equal weight to his admission that he and his parents didn't get along, yet she didn't flinch, didn't mind talking about something that must have been at least somewhat painful.

"How old were you when you assumed the responsibility for your house?"

She paused, considered. "I think fourteen. My parents simply couldn't make ends meet anymore. There were eight of us, you see, and when you multiplied everything by eight there never was enough money to go around."

"So your mother got a job."

Her attention focused on Lacy as she fed her the vegetables and spaghetti she'd mashed with a fork, Madison nodded.

"And you got the family."

"Something like that," Madison agreed casually.

"You can't tell me you weren't bitter," Ryan said, irritated that she seemed so cool about this.

"Not really bitter. Simply determined that I'd never be poor again, that no one in my family would ever have to live counting every penny."

All right, Ryan thought. He was getting the picture now. "So, you don't like to cook anymore."

She shook her head. "I love to cook," she contradicted, peering at him over the rim of her wineglass. It amazed him that she could not only feed herself and her child, but she could also carry on a conversation—without spilling a drop—and still look incredibly beautiful.

"I also love to dust and set a pretty table," she said, once more turning her attention to Lacy. "But doing those things always reminded me of being poor, being without money." She sighed, set Lacy's fork on her plate and looked Ryan right in the eye. "Yesterday you helped me to see that I've been running from that without even knowing it."

"You didn't know you didn't like being poor?"

Madison laughed. "Oh, I knew I didn't like being poor. What I didn't realize was that I'd deprived myself of things I really loved…like cooking…because it reminded me of being poor." She stopped, combed her fingers through her hair. "I'm not making any sense."

"Oh, no," Ryan disagreed, shaking his head. "You're making perfect sense. I felt the same way at Angus's. For the longest time I couldn't stand doing some of the chores, but I didn't know why. After I graduated from college, Pete

Samuels, the old sheriff, retired and I took his job—no questions asked—just to get off the ranch.''

"What happened?"

"After a year or two of working as sheriff, getting an identity so to speak, I realized I could help Angus and Cal, and even enjoy it. That was when I knew it wasn't the work, but remembering feelings because of the work that drove me crazy. Those stupid chores reminded me of being on the edge, always wondering if I'd be there tomorrow or if something would force me to leave because of my pride."

"But you still want to be sheriff?"

Shaking his head, Ryan chuckled. "I love the ranch, but I'm not a rancher. Cal's a rancher. The land's in his blood. I'm more of a people person."

"Because you understand them."

"On some levels, yeah. I guess I do."

"Then you'll understand when I tell you that your suggestion yesterday had me thinking about more than cooking," she said, feeding Lacy a bite of food. "I've decided to take Lacy out in public with me."

Ryan set his fork on his plate. "What?"

"Well, when I considered the future, about how she'd feel that I left her every time I had a publicity function or charity function, I started to see that though I couldn't always have her go with me, there were certain places she could go with me.

"The thing was, taking her with me would mean bringing her out into the world. Introducing her."

"And?" Ryan asked cautiously.

"And I didn't get frightened like I used to when I thought about it."

"What about the fact that you want Lacy to live a normal life?"

"*Normal* is a relative term. Since she's my daughter,

Lacy's life isn't going to be the same as most children's, but it will be the life she knows, and for her that life will be normal.''

In his mind's eye, Ryan could see it, understand it.

''That's not to say this is going to be easy. As she grows, there'll be a lot of work to be done. For instance, I think she should always know where I go and what I do. In a sense, she's a stakeholder in my company, if only from the perspective that this company is what takes most of her mommy's time. That's why I think she should come to the office with me periodically, so she can see it and understand it as much as she can, in order to understand where I am and what I'm doing.''

Unimpressed, Ryan picked up his fork again. ''I guess that makes sense.''

''Well, it doesn't make a lot of sense alone, but when you combine that with the fact that I now know that I need to spend a lot more time at home, and that's the other half of the work we need to do, then it does make sense. In fact, it changes everything.''

Ryan's fork stopped halfway to his mouth. ''You're going to start spending more time at home?''

''There are lots of ways for me to spend more time at home. First, I can work at my house. I can do a great deal of my creative work in my own den, which means I need go into the office solely for meetings and crises.''

''This is a hell of a change of heart you're having here, Madison.''

''Yeah, I suppose when you consider it from your vantage point it may seem that way.''

He stared at her. ''Is there another vantage point?''

This time she stopped, caught his gaze. ''I want to make a home, Ryan. I want to buy knickknacks, I want to match my curtains. I want to care about my china pattern.''

His throat went dry. ''You're kidding.''

"I couldn't be more serious. I'm done running. I know what I want now." She stopped, caught his gaze. "I want a home."

As far as Ryan was concerned, the world came to a crashing halt. He knew she knew exactly what she was saying, what she was offering. "Are you sure?" he whispered, mesmerized by the possibilities.

"I couldn't be more sure."

Ryan got the feeling that everything he wanted was within reach of his tingling fingers. Over Lacy's noisy protests, he slid the fork from Madison's fingers and set it on her plate. Then he leaned over and pressed his mouth against hers. Heat enveloped him immediately, along with an overwhelming sense of need. He'd known this woman less than two weeks, yet he wanted her more than he'd ever wanted anyone. It didn't seem right, it didn't seem possible.

He pulled back. He wasn't sure he could trust it, or himself, particularly not now that she'd erased his last vestige of protest. He had to think about this. He had to think long and hard about this.

And so did she.

"What would you say if I told you I need some time to get used to the new you?"

She tilted her head. "I'd say you were pretty smart and also within your rights."

He pushed his chair away from the table. "Since you cooked, you can leave the dishes for me."

"Where are you going?"

"Just out," he said, sounding both confused and amazed. "I won't go far, I promise, but I need to go."

Madison watched him walk out the door, her stomach churning with a combination of relief and regret. She hadn't exactly expected him to ask her to marry him, but she didn't expect him to leave, either.

Before she could take her thoughts any further, the phone

rang. After quickly securing Lacy, she ran to answer it.
"Hello," she said breathlessly.

"What are you doing that has you out of breath?" Jessica asked with a laugh.

"Nothing. I had to run for the phone."

"That cabin's not big enough to have to run for the phone."

"I had to settle Lacy before I could start running. What's up?"

"Nothing. At least nothing pertaining to you. I do need to talk with Ryan, though."

"He just left. He's out in the woods somewhere."

"Oh, no. Did you two have another fight?"

Madison controlled the smile that began to bloom. "No," she said, but the word came out in one long, happy note.

"Oh, great, this doesn't sound good, either."

"It should. We're in a truce of sorts. I guess you could say I made him an offer, and he's now outside thinking about it."

"After our last conversation, I'm not sure I trust you offering him anything."

"Jess, stop teasing me. I think I'm finally in love for the first time in my life," she said, and realized instantly it was true. The knowledge poured over her, wafted through her and warmed her all over. She was in love. Really in love. And it was different, so different from what she'd believed it would be that she felt nearly overwhelmed. "The least you can do is take it seriously."

There was a short pause before Jessica said, "Oh, honey, I take it very seriously, because not only are you my friend, but Ryan is my friend. And the two of you together, as far as I'm concerned, are nothing but trouble."

Offended, Madison plopped into an available chair. "Why?"

"We talked about this before, Madison. The two of you aren't merely different, Ryan has some painful scars from parents who had a lifestyle very much likes yours."

"I'm changing my lifestyle."

Another pause. A soft, quiet "What?"

"I've decided to rearrange my life. I'm going to change things. I'm going to make him the home he wants."

"How?"

"By cutting back on my schedule and doing most of my creating at home."

"Madison, didn't you try this when Lacy was born?"

Chewing her lower lip, Madison remembered she had. "Yes."

"And what makes this time different?"

"I have better motivation."

"Better than a brand-new baby?"

"Things were different then," Madison insisted.

"Maybe," Jessica agreed softly. "And maybe things seem different because you've been away from the pressures of your office for almost two weeks." Jessica paused, sighed. "Maddy, things always look different—better— away from the chaos. I know your intentions are good, but even with the best of intentions you may be making promises, commitments, that you can't keep."

Chapter Thirteen

After eliciting a promise that Madison wouldn't do anything foolish, Jessica explained that she needed to speak with Ryan and might drive up again the following day. Madison knew she would. And she almost didn't blame her. Madison and Ryan were two of Jessica's best friends. She didn't want to see them make a mistake.

"It isn't just your hurting Ryan that worries me," Jessica had said before she disconnected the call. "I'm worried about you, too. Before Lacy that business was your life. Now you're telling me you're going to be able to pull back, to change the way you work. It's all a little too hard for me to believe."

Madison saw her point, but a part of her was annoyed at Jessica's interference. Still, the next morning when Jessica arrived, dressed as usual in a striking suit, yellow this time, with matching handbag and shoes, she picked up Lacy to cuddle her, and all of Madison's irritation melted away. This woman was her best friend. This woman knew her better than she knew herself sometimes. Madison realized that Jessica's intentions were nothing but good, and her warnings weren't to be taken lightly.

Nonetheless, when Jessica told Madison she didn't have time to wait for Ryan to decide to appear from the forest, Madison jumped at the chance to go after him.

"By yourself?"

"Sure," Madison said. "Why not?"

"I don't know, but I sure as hell wouldn't want to go out in the woods alone."

"He can't be far. He told me he never goes far, that he can still see the cabin."

Jessica's brow puckered. "And you'll come back if you can't find him in ten minutes?"

"Scout's honor!" Madison said, crossing her heart.

Jessica peered down at her banana yellow pumps. "All right. Better you than me."

Sighing with relief over the opportunity to leave the cabin without taking Lacy with her, Madison ran down the plank steps. The forest was alive with sounds and scents and sights. Vivid greens, woody browns, patches of blue sky peeking through the trees. Remembering what Ryan had said about always being able to see the cabin, she chose the path that seemed to lead to a clearing of some sort. She walked only a short distance before she heard the sound of rushing water. Intrigued, she quickened her pace, all thoughts of Ryan forgotten.

The trail took a sharp turn. Madison rounded the curve and gasped with delight. There in the middle of nowhere and nothing was a waterfall. The narrow stream of water tumbled into a pool that formed a nearly perfect circle, the overflow spilling into a small brook. Trees sheltered the grotto. Wildflowers sprouted indiscriminately, providing a chaotic beauty that was both innocent and wild.

"I come here to think."

At the sound of Ryan's voice, Madison spun around, palm pressed to her chest.

"You scared the life out of me."

"You woke me from a perfectly wonderful nap," he countered, as if that made them even.

She glanced around. Not seeing a sleeping bag or mat or a blanket, she looked over at him. "You sleep out here?"

"I awaken a lot during the night." He paused, shrugged. "I check on you. It's my job."

But Madison sensed it was more than his job. In the few seconds that passed, a thousand different realizations raced through her head. That he protected her, liked her, went to such extremes to ensure not merely that she was safe, but that she didn't realize how much effort he put into her safety.

"And you feel you have to hide that from me?"

"Just because I don't tell you something, doesn't mean I'm hiding it from you."

Realizing what he said was true, Madison said nothing. Water toppled behind them, echoing through the silence. The sweet scent of wet earth enveloped them. Colors surrounded them. In Madison's lifetime she'd seen no spot more perfect, more beautiful. Before Ryan knew about Lacy, he'd told her that this could end up being something like a vacation for her, and suddenly, clearly, she knew what he meant.

"You ever swim in that pool?"

He shrugged. "Sometimes."

She shielded her eyes from a strong beam of sunlight that found its way into the alcove between two trees. "Wanna swim now?"

Obviously torn, he glanced around. "Where's Lacy?"

She smiled. "With Jessica."

"Jessica's here?"

"She needs to talk with you about something pertaining

to another of your cases. It must not be important, though, since she said if I didn't find you she'd see you at the courthouse when I go to testify.''

"It could be one of three or four different things...."

Madison poked his arm. "You wanna swim or not?"

Ryan gave her a pained look. "Do you realize what you're saying?"

"Yeah, I'm asking you to have a little break with me. To do something fun for a change. Are you in or not?"

"Madison," he explained patiently, the tormented expression still on his face. "We don't have suits. We'd have to swim naked."

"Or in our clothes," Madison pointed out logically. "You take off your shirt, and your cutoff jeans are perfectly acceptable swimwear. And I've swum in a T-shirt and shorts before, too." She kicked off her tennis shoes. "I was one of eight kids, remember? I'm quite accustomed to making do." When she saw she hadn't quite convinced him, she smiled wickedly. "Unless you're a coward who can't swim."

"It's not nice to call somebody names," he said, then pushed her into the pool.

She fell into the water and came up sputtering. "It's not nice to push somebody into the water without any warning."

"I simply wanted to prove to you that the water isn't deep, so there's nothing to be afraid of," he said, then jumped into the pool the way a kid would, feet first. "You can't dive," he explained, swimming over to her. "And the water is very cold."

"I didn't get a chance to notice."

"Complaining?" he asked, grinning.

She splashed him. "I know better. It wouldn't do any good."

"You're right," he agreed, and picked her up. She

screamed, but as her protest echoed around them, he tossed her into the water again.

"You're enjoying this!" she yelped, exploding out of the waves that rippled around her.

"Of course I am," he said, laughing. "Do you know how long it's been since I played in this pool?"

"Don't tell me you used to do this to poor Grace."

"Nope," Ryan said, then he grinned again. "But her friends were fair game."

"You're impossible!" Madison said, when he began to approach her again. "And I'm staying away from you!"

"Why? Because you can't have fun, don't want to have fun or don't know how to have fun?"

His question sounded so exactly on par with the accusations Jessica had made that Madison's spine stiffened. "Why does everyone think I don't know how to have fun?"

"Do you?"

"Of course, I do."

"Then do something fun. Do a somersault in the water or something."

The devil came to her, and pretending to do exactly what he'd suggested, she cut into the water. But instead of turning herself over, she lunged forward, grabbed his ankle and toppled him. As he went under, she splashed out.

A few seconds later he propelled himself to the surface. Over the sputtering and choking, she saw the fire of revenge light his blue eyes. "You've had it now."

"Oh, you didn't like that?" she teased, walking backward away from him. "Would this be a little case of being able to dish it out but not being able to take it?"

"Wait. Stop, Madison," he said, suddenly serious. "There's a drop-off back there somewhere, we can only stay in the center of the pool."

"Yeah, right," she said, still inching backward. "You

think I was born yesterday, or that no guys tried that trick on me in the creek outside of my hometown?''

"I'm sure plenty of guys tried plenty of tricks on you, but right now I'm not teasing,'' Ryan said, but instead of his words winning her over, she hastened her pace. "Stop. I mean it.''

She heard the "Stop,'' but the "I mean it,'' came about three seconds too late. The silt beneath her feet suddenly became nothing. She heard the hollow sound of being submerged, and she swallowed water before realizing what had happened. By then she was already in significant trouble; she had to struggle to stop from plunging deeper and didn't have enough concentration left to push herself to the top again.

At that moment Ryan's arms came around her. He pulled her up to the surface and propelled her to the shallow end of the pool within a matter of seconds. Every bit as quickly, he picked her up again and threw her out of the lagoon onto a bed of soft grass, then he landed beside her.

He patted her back as she gasped for air. "Try and cough out the water you might have swallowed or breathed in,'' he instructed.

Madison gasped, "I'm fine.'' She took several long, deep breaths then added, "I wasn't under that long.''

"Because I saw you going.''

"Well, if you hadn't been teasing me, acting like a damned fool…''

"Who started this?'' Ryan demanded, glaring at her. "If I remember correctly, it all started when you teased me about being afraid to go into the water because I couldn't swim.''

"And then *you* pushed me,'' Madison said, falling onto her back and closing her eyes because, foolishly, she was getting angry now. "Teasing someone about being a coward isn't equal to pushing them into the water. Pushing is an actual physical act…'' She opened her eyes to finish her sentence, but the words died in her throat.

Ryan was looking down at her, as irritated with her as she was with him, his face a mere six inches away. But when she opened her eyes, and her gaze fastened on his, the expression on his face changed, softened.

''Are you sure you're all right?'' he asked quietly.

She swallowed the lump in her throat. ''Yeah, I'm fine.''

''Good,'' he said, then bent his head and kissed her. As if aggravated by the thought that he'd almost lost her, Ryan kissed her greedily, hungrily.

Warm waves of delight wafted over her, leaving the tug and pull of arousal in their wake. Desire hit her so quickly and so hard she was momentarily stunned. The only thing she could do was react. Her arms circled him, her palms finding the sinewy muscle of his back and shoulders. Her lips opened to him, inviting him, teasing him, coaxing him.

But he didn't need much persuasion. He was taking, possessing. ''You said the baby is with Jessica?'' he asked against her mouth.

''Yes.''

''She's safe and happy?''

''She loves Jessica.''

''That's all I wanted to know.'' He took her mouth as if it were his right, his tongue thrusting between her lips, as his hands began a frenzied exploration of her body. He didn't pause anyplace long enough for her to recognize a specific sensation. Instead, feelings flooded through her. Longing surged and crested, becoming desire. Desire swirled like a tornado until it became arousal. He took her higher and higher, much easier than she imagined was possible, much faster than she knew was advisable.

Still, she was a grown woman, a consenting adult. Ryan was, too. She'd waited all her life to find him, it seemed, and almost two long weeks before they could find an acceptable compromise that allowed them to get this close. They'd fought this hunger for two long weeks. She wanted everything, and she wanted it now. No matter what Jessica said about being careful, being cautious.

The very second she thought about Jessica her entire body seemed to freeze. Things were moving too quickly. Not because they weren't ready, but more because Madison had made promises she wasn't sure she could keep.

She pulled her mouth away from his, then swallowed hard. "I think maybe we're getting a little ahead of ourselves here."

"I think we're making up for lost time," he disagreed, then kissed her again.

Difficult though it was to tug herself away from his full, soft mouth, Madison did, anyway. "We haven't known each other long enough to go where I think you're taking us."

He stopped. "You're serious."

"I couldn't be more serious."

He seemed to ponder that for several minutes, then he pushed himself away from her. "You're right."

"And you're not angry?" she asked, knowing that even if he was, she wouldn't know what to say to talk him out of it. She certainly wouldn't tell him that she questioned her ability to keep her commitment to change her work style. That would only reenforce his initial fears. No, she really couldn't tell him anything.

He shook his head. "How can I be angry with you for using common sense?"

"I don't know," she said, smiling slightly as she shrugged her shoulders.

He drew a long breath, then, leaning back, he stared up at the bright blue sky for several seconds before returning his gaze to hers. "But I'm not a patient man. I think we both know this is right. Don't play games with me, Madison. I can't handle that."

"I'm not. And I won't," she quickly assured him, then wondered if playing games wasn't just what she was doing. She had to get back to town. She had to get back to work. She had to get back to her normal life to prove to him and herself that she could do everything she promised. Because if she made love with him before that, there'd be no backing out. Not for him or for her.

And she would have a choice. Hurt him or completely change her life to suit him. Because if her present plan didn't work, there was no compromise for them. They were either together on his terms or together on hers. And he'd already made it very clear he wouldn't accept her terms.

Chapter Fourteen

"Madison fell into the pool and I had to rescue her."

Ryan answered Jessica's gasp when, dripping wet, they walked into the main room of Angus's cabin.

"Good glory, girl, are you okay?"

"I'm fine," Madison said, but though the lie helped them get through an awkward situation, Madison felt odd that Ryan had used a cover story rather than tell Jessica the truth.

"I think I'll go upstairs and change," Madison said, not caring to delve too deeply into Ryan's motives. Not now. They'd finally come to an agreement that worked for both of them, and she wasn't ruining it with suspicion.

As she walked away, Ryan directed Jessica to the front porch. "I use that waterfall for my morning shower," he said, holding the screen door open for Jessica who exited before him. "This time I happened to have laundered my clothing, too." Before he stepped outside, Ryan turned and winked at Madison, and she felt her bones liquify. What that man could do to her with just a look, just a wink, was unbelievable.

If this wasn't love, she didn't have a clue what was.

After changing her clothes and putting Lacy down for a morning nap, Madison took her wet T-shirt and jeans downstairs with her. There was one place to hang them for drying and that was across the rail of the front porch.

She didn't want to disturb Jessica and Ryan, but she felt she didn't have a choice. When she pushed open the screen door, she discovered Jessica had already gone. Ryan sat alone on the old wooden swing.

"She needed to clarify a few statements I made on a police report," Ryan explained, as Madison arranged her jeans over the railing. "She said she tried to call, but I was out and she decided to drive up here instead."

"Must be pretty important stuff."

"Actually, it's dry, dull, routine stuff. No reason for her to come up here at all." He paused. "What did you tell her that has her so scared to leave us unattended that she's always driving up here to check on us?" he asked, unwittingly answering Madison's question about why he'd lied to Jessica. He hadn't been withholding the truth as much as he had been trying to preserve Jessica's sanity.

"Nothing," Madison hedged. "Well, not really *nothing, nothing*, but nothing important."

"Oh, that made sense," Ryan said. Hearing the laughter in his voice, Madison faced him, and at the same moment he grabbed her wrist and tumbled her to his lap.

She squealed. "Your shorts are still wet."

The devil was in his eyes. "So?"

"Now my clean jeans are going to be wet!"

"Take them off. You can lay them across the rail with the other pair and they'll stay nice and dry."

"Fat chance," she said with a giggle, and tried to wiggle off his thighs. For a few seconds he fought her, then he let her go. The minute she was away from him, she wished she hadn't fought that hard.

"I'm sorry," she said miserably. "I'm having a little trouble getting used to us liking each other."

He exhaled a long sigh. "And I promised I wouldn't push you." Leaning back on the old swing, he closed his eyes. "But there isn't a whole hell of a lot for us to do up here to get to know each other."

"Oh, I don't know," Madison said, sitting on the top step of the porch. "We've gone swimming. We've played board games. You've seen me work. You've seen me at my best...with my baby."

"And you've seen me at my best, like the other night when I protected you from the bouncing soda can."

The memory had her smiling. "In spite of the way you belittle your job, I know you like what you do."

"Of course I do, or I wouldn't be doing it."

Knowing with unequivocal certainty that that was true, Madison settled herself against the post that supported the overhanging roof. "It's beautiful out here. Peaceful."

"Angus loves it."

"I bet he does." She paused, considered, then faced Ryan. "So how did he end up with three kids who aren't his?"

Ryan shrugged. "Well, you know most of my story. My parents let Angus have a shot at raising me when they couldn't find a boarding school that would accept me."

She nodded.

"Grace and Cal were the children of a ranch hand who fell ill and died."

"And Angus decided to raise them, no questions asked?"

"Not exactly, but just about," Ryan said. "When Jackson, Cal and Grace's dad, went from being an outside man to being one of the inside people, he and Cal and Grace moved into the house. I lived with Angus in the main part of the house, but Angus didn't like me being alone—or maybe singled out is a better way to phrase it—so he had Cal and Grace and their father eat with us. Angus took Grace and Cal to church with us. He even took them along when we shopped for school clothes. All to sort of make me feel like I wasn't alone.''

Madison smiled. "Did it work?"

Ryan grinned. "I think better than he wanted it to work. Before he knew what was happening, he was refereeing fights, going to parent-teacher conferences and volunteering his cook's services for bake sales."

Madison laughed. "You'd think he'd have better respect for his cooks then."

"You would, wouldn't you."

"That's an amazing story," Madison said, settling more comfortably against the post.

"Not really. That's Angus. He always jumps in and does what needs to be done. Unfortunately he comes across as being nosy and overbearing, but you have to know how to take him."

"I guess Cal and Grace's father didn't mind that Angus commandeered his kids."

"In a sense I think Jackson hung on as long as he did for Cal and Grace. Once he knew Angus would care for them, I think he felt as if he finally had permission to die."

"Permission to die?" Madison gasped.

Ryan nodded. "He'd been sick for a long time. Every-body thought he was a drinker…and he was. But he drank because he was in a lot of pain. Some days getting drunk was the only way he could handle it."

Not knowing what else to say, Madison sympathetically shook her head.

"Cal and Grace took his death really hard. As far as they knew, they had no family but their father. Turns out, they had an aunt or a cousin or something in Ohio, but she was a virtual stranger. I never saw two people who looked so alone or lonely. So I kind of took them under my wing, didn't let anybody pick on them at school, didn't let the hands tease Cal.''

She could see him. In her mind's eye she could see Ryan defending Grace and Cal, protecting them, taking care of them. It was no wonder he ended up as a small-town sheriff. He was a natural.

''Angus adopted Grace, since she wasn't quite sixteen when Jackson died. But Cal was eighteen. Angus didn't need to adopt him, and Cal didn't seem to want to be adopted. Cal didn't want anything except the chance to keep working on the ranch. Angus gave it to him.''

''I had to go to college. Angus wouldn't let me throw away everything my parents wanted me to have, and the only way he could figure out to make damned sure I'd realize what I was losing was to force me to get a degree in business.''

''You're kidding?'' Madison said, pleasantly surprised.

''Nope, and I didn't get my degree by the skin of my teeth, either. I buckled down, studied hard and always made the dean's list, just to make sure everybody realized giving up the American dream was my *choice,* not an act of God.''

The way he said that gave Madison a run of chills down her spine. His strong belief that he was right about the kind of life he picked was something she was not going to change about him, and a reminder that she was going to have to do the bigger half of the compromising.

''You told me we weren't very far from a town,'' she said, thinking out loud, ready to reenforce her commitments as best she could given the circumstances.

''We're not,'' he agreed carefully.

''Well, how about if I give you a shopping list and I'll make us a wonderful dinner tonight.''

''Like what?'' he asked skeptically.

"How about grilled chicken and fettuccine Alfredo with mushrooms?"

"You can make that?"

"Not only can I make that, but I can make the low-cal, low-fat version."

Ryan glanced down at his spare frame. "Why are you always trying to feed me low-fat food?"

"I'm watching your cholesterol because I like you," she said, rose and planted a soft kiss on his lips. "I want you to be around for a long, long time."

Her answer must have pleased him because he grinned, grabbed her wrist and pulled her back for a longer, more-satisfying kiss. "You make the list. I'll warm up the Bronco."

When Ryan returned from the store, he gave Madison her supplies, and she chased him out of the kitchen. But the second he reached the doorway, Lacy began to wail.

He stopped.

Madison stopped.

Both looked over at Lacy.

"Go on," Madison said. "I'll get her."

"Why not let me get her?"

His suggestion seemed to confuse her. "You want to?"

"Madison, she's cute as a bug's ear. Of course I want to."

"No, that's okay I'll—" Lacy interrupted her with another loud wail.

"I think even she wants me to take her outside."

Madison chewed her bottom lip. "Are you sure?"

"Yes, I'm sure. And Lacy's sure," Ryan said, lifting Lacy from her high chair. "Why is her mother unsure?"

"I don't know, I guess it's because I have to be away from her all the time, and I don't like to give her up when I do get to spend time with her."

"I'd say that's a pretty good indication that it might be time that you trimmed your work schedule."

He said it calmly, casually, but he held his breath, waiting for her reply.

"I'd already told you I was going to," she said, then shooed him and Lacy out of the kitchen.

Ryan felt his heart swell with hope. Every time he tested her, she passed. Somewhere in the recesses of his soul, he knew that this little interlude in the cabin had been preordained not only to bring them together, but also to show her she needed to slow down.

Things were going to work out. He could sense it. He could *feel* it.

As long as she could put her work second, nothing, but nothing, would separate them again.

And so far she'd passed every test.

Madison was awakened by a loud banging on the cabin door. Before she got her legs out from under the covers, she heard the sound of Ryan's feet pounding along the hall and then down the steps.

Slowly, cautiously, she got out of bed. She knew somebody sent to kill her wouldn't knock. So she soothed Lacy back to sleep, then tiptoed down the steps just as Ryan opened the door.

"What are you doing here?"

"Madison," Jessica said, speaking around Ryan to Madison who had stepped into the main room. "I'm afraid I have some bad news. One of your factories burned down tonight."

"Oh, my God," Madison said, and pressed her fingers to her lips before collapsing on the sofa. "What happened?"

"No one knows," Jessica said. "But Joe Turner got me out of bed tonight because I'm your best friend, and he figured if anybody would know where you were, I would. I told him I couldn't tell him where you were, but I'd have you call him. He asked that you make it as soon as possible."

"I never trained my staff to take over for me," Madison explained, though her voice sounded accusing, even to herself. "They don't know what to do without me. I've never let anyone make big decisions on their own. I'm not surprised Joe won't fill out a fire insurance form without my approval."

"Filling out insurance forms is the least of Joe's worries," Jessica said, easing into the room. "There was a night crew working in the factory that burned. Two people were seriously injured. They're in the hospital."

Disbelief hit Madison like a paralyzing wave. She had to absorb the information and process it, before she could rise from the couch. "I have to go back. I can't give instructions to you for how my people should handle this. *I* have to go back and handle it."

"What if the fire was set to bring you out into the open?" Ryan asked quietly.

"I can't have workers in the hospital and not be available."

"Not even if it means that visiting those workers gets you killed?" he demanded.

"He's right, Madison," Jessica said gently. "There hasn't been a determination of the origin of the fire. It might have been arson. And that means the fire might have been set to flush you out."

"The hell with that," Madison said, her temper exploding. "I have workers in the hospital. I have other workers who are now out of a job. They'll be waking up tomorrow morning wondering how they're going to pay their bills. I have responsibilities to these people."

"You also have responsibilities to Lacy," Ryan coolly reminded. "And to me."

"Right at this minute, my responsibility is to my workers," Madison stated evenly. Ryan's reaction to that statement immediately registered in his facial expression. "Ryan, the odds are that I'm not going to be killed. The odds are someone dropped a cigarette in the wrong place, or an electrical wire shorted out. The odds are that there's an explanation for that fire. And all those workers, the injured ones and the ones wondering if they're going to have a job tomorrow, they all need to know that I'm going to make everything right for them."

Without waiting for Ryan's response, Madison said, "I want you to drive me to the hospital."

"Okay," Jessica agreed.

Ryan cursed.

Madison ignored him and continued speaking. "We can use your car phone to call Mrs. Phillips, and let her know I'm bringing Lacy over."

"Agreed," Jessica said, nodding.

Ryan grabbed Madison's arm and spun her around to face him. "I can't stop you from risking your own life. You're an adult. But I won't let you risk Lacy."

Madison closed her eyes; when she opened them they were filled with steely determination. "Ryan, I don't have time to argue with you."

"I don't want to argue," Ryan calmly returned. "I just want to take Lacy to Angus's ranch."

"That would actually be safer," Jessica interjected. "And don't think you're going to be running around unescorted, either. Since you'll be out in the open and since this situation may be dangerous, I'm hiring a professional."

Madison thought for a second. "All right. You're right,"

she said, turning to Ryan. ''You can take Lacy to Angus's ranch.''

He skewered her with a look that could have crumbled concrete. ''Thanks for the permission.''

Chapter Fifteen

It was only four forty-five when Ryan drove up to the ranch house, but Angus ran out to meet him.

"What in the heck are you doing home?" he asked as Ryan opened the door to his Bronco. "I thought that trial wasn't scheduled until two days from now."

"There's been a change in plans," Ryan said, unfolding his tall frame as he got out of the vehicle. "I couldn't stop Madison from running off to hold the hands of some corporate executives, but I refused to leave Lacy in the custody of somebody I didn't know."

Ryan watched Angus digest that information before he peeked into the vehicle to see the baby who was sound asleep in her brightly colored car seat.

"Oh, my sweet Lord," he whispered reverently. "If she isn't the most beautiful child God created, then He may strike me dead right at this minute."

Ryan gave Lacy a loving smile. "She gets cuter as the days go on, Angus. If you think she's beautiful now, you're going to be head over heels in love by the time she goes back to her mother."

"I'll take my chances," Angus said, unlatched the belt of the car seat, then removed the padded bar. "I'll carry her in, and we'll see what we can do about sleeping accommodations."

"Not to worry," Ryan said, watching Angus cradle Lacy, quickly and efficiently lifting her from her car seat. "Not only do I have a fold-away crib in here," Ryan continued, as he walked around the back of the Bronco. "But I've got a play yard, swing and high chair...all in the brightest shades of red, blue, green and yellow imaginable."

"That oughta please Cal."

"What oughta please Cal?" Cal asked, jogging down the three steps of the wooden porch. "Well, would you look at her."

"That's Madison's little girl."

Cal said nothing, merely lifted an eyebrow in question as he peered at Ryan.

"Somebody set fire to one of the Kidtastic factories. It seems Madison's corporate whiz kids couldn't manage without her."

"And you got custody of the baby," Cal speculated, giving Ryan a knowing look.

"I refused to let Madison shuffle Lacy off to her nanny's house," Ryan corrected, and slammed the lid of the back of his Bronco after all of Lacy's things were stacked on the ground behind it. "I was ordered to protect Madison and Lacy. Madison's old enough to choose to refuse my protection. Lacy's not. In the end Jessica saw things my way."

With that Ryan grabbed the folded high chair and swing and bounded up the steps. When he was nearly at the front door of the ranch house he heard Angus whisper, "Loves the child, he does. In a roundabout way he admitted it to me. I don't think he's admitted it to himself though."

Ryan heard Cal mutter something, but he didn't bother

to argue. It didn't matter what he felt about Lacy. Her mother had proven beyond a shadow of a doubt that she didn't have the time in her life, or the inclination, to give a relationship priority. That hurt so much that Ryan not only didn't want to deal with it, he actually didn't think he could right now.

"Are you bringing the kid or not?" he called testily as he pushed his way into the foyer.

"I'm right behind you," Angus whispered, and when Ryan turned around Angus made shushing sounds and batted his free hand to indicate Ryan should hold the noise down.

Cal walked in carrying the portable crib and the play yard. "Where do you want these?"

"Leave the play yard down here," Ryan said, then started up the steps. "But bring the crib up to my room."

Cal and Angus peeked at each other.

"You're going to care for her by yourself?" Cal asked skeptically.

Ryan stopped on the steps and faced them. "Do *you* want to?" he asked Cal.

Grinning, Cal shook his head. "I wouldn't know the first thing about tending to a child."

"Well, I happen to have learned a good bit over the past two weeks."

Cal glanced at Angus, and Angus nodded that Cal should obey Ryan's directive. Leaving the play yard in the foyer, Cal grabbed the crib and began following Ryan up the steps. Rocking Lacy to make sure she stayed in a nice, comfortable sleep, Angus took up the rear.

Per instructions neatly printed on the side of the crib, Ryan had it standing and secure in a matter of minutes. He stretched a fitted sheet over the mattress, then slid Lacy from Angus's arms and settled her in bed.

"There. If she's consistent, she won't awaken until about

nine," Ryan said, then turned to Angus and Cal who were both gazing at the little blond baby as if she were an angel straight from heaven. "I'd love some breakfast."

Angus frowned at him. "Now?"

"Well, it is morning," Ryan pointed out.

"Go fix yourself an egg," Cal said without taking his eyes off Lacy.

"Eggs have too much cholesterol."

That got Angus's attention. "Since when have you cared?"

"And how did you figure that out?" Cal added as both Angus and Cal stared at Ryan dubiously.

Ryan threw his hands up in defeat. "Never mind," he said, storming to the door. "I'll go fix myself a piece of wheat toast."

"Wheat toast?" Cal mouthed to Angus, who shrugged his shoulders in reply.

"I'd say we're going to have a very interesting story unfolding here," Angus said, then kissed the tips of his fingers before pressing them to Lacy's forehead. "Let's go down and badger him some more. See if we can't get the real scoop."

Cal grinned. "My pleasure."

Angus couldn't resist calling Grace, but when she arrived, Ryan was furious. "Do you think I'm not capable of caring for a child?" he demanded, watching from the living room window as Grace ran up the steps to the front door.

"Not at all," Angus replied casually. "I simply think Grace should have the opportunity to play with Lacy, too."

"Where is she?" Grace said as she plowed into the foyer.

"We have her in here," Angus called, then rose and

greeted Grace with a kiss on the cheek. "That is if you can wrestle her away from Ryan."

"You didn't need to come," Ryan groused. "Between the three of us we can certainly tend to one child for two days."

"And you're going to," Grace agreed, scooping Lacy from his arms. "Oh, Lord, she's so sweet," she gasped as she lifted Lacy into the air and Lacy giggled playfully.

Ryan narrowed his eyes at Grace. "If you're not here to help, then why are you here?"

"Look around you, Ryan," Grace said with a laugh. "There are no babies. There haven't been any babies since the kids of that one housekeeper you scared off a few Februaries ago. Anytime any one of us gets a chance to see a baby, we grab it."

"Well, since the two of you will have that child occupied for the next several days," Angus said sarcastically, "I'm going to go see if Cal needs a hand."

Though Grace casually settled Lacy onto her lap, and equally casually asked, "Are you sure you're feeling up to it?" Ryan saw the way she tensed when Angus mentioned going out to work with Cal.

"Of course I'm up to it," Angus muttered, walking to the front door. "And I don't need a mother," he added, as he grabbed his Stetson from the hook by the door. "Get all that out of your system with Lacy and then I'll be back for dinner."

With that he left the house, slamming the door behind him.

Grace glanced at Ryan. "I think that's why he called me. He's tired of me mothering him."

Shaking his head, Ryan laughed. "Nope. I think you just got stuck with making dinner."

"Damn!" Grace said. "I didn't even see that coming."

"Well, if you wouldn't mind putting Lacy down for her

nap now," Ryan said, glancing at his watch. "I'd be happy to help you."

Unhappy, Grace grimaced. "Is it time?"

"According to my schedule it is."

She sighed. "All right. I'll play with her after dinner."

"Fair enough," Ryan said, then gripped Lacy and pulled her from Grace's arms. "This will only take me a minute."

"And that'll give me time to see what Angus has in the kitchen."

"If he were smart, he'd have a cook," Ryan said, walking to the staircase.

"Fired him last week," Grace said with a wince. "I think he simply doesn't like strangers in the house. Either that or he likes *your* cooking."

"Or *your* cooking," Ryan said, taking the first step cautiously. "Or your *company*," he added meaningfully.

Grace sighed. "We're going to have to talk to him about that," she said, then started for the kitchen.

Ryan met her about ten minutes later. "Went out like a light."

"You're very good with her," Grace observed indifferently as she began to peel a potato. "Jump in here anytime you want," she offered to Ryan, motioning to the potatoes.

"What are we making?"

"Beef stew," Grace said. "Because those were the ingredients I found first."

Ryan shrugged. "Hey, whatever works."

They peeled potatoes in silence for about a minute before Grace said, "So, aren't you going to tell me about why Lacy's here?"

"Didn't Angus tell you?"

"He said something about a fire at one of the Kidtastic factories, but that was it. That was all he told me."

"That might be because that's all there is to tell."

"Oh, come on, Ryan," Grace groaned. "I saw the way you act with that kid."

Ryan stopped peeling. "If you're implying that I like Lacy a little more than normal, you're right."

Grace groaned again. "Don't go all macho and spacey on me, Ryan. This is me. Grace. Surrogate sister. I know something's happening here." She stopped, looked at Ryan. "No, better yet, I know you need to talk to somebody. So, don't pretend you don't. I'm here. Talk."

"Is this why Angus called you?" he asked moodily.

She shook her head. "Angus would much rather have you spill your guts to him, than me."

Her admission broke some of the tension and Ryan laughed. "You're right," he agreed, then shook his head. "I don't know where to start."

"Start by telling me where Madison is."

He stiffened. "I'm not quite sure. All I know is that Jessica came to the cabin last night with the news of the fire. She told Madison that two employees were hospitalized, and Madison felt she had to make at least one trip to the hospital to assure them that they had her support."

Grace tossed a peeled potato into the bowl of cool water. "I understand that."

Ryan gave her a puzzled frown. "Do you?"

"Of course," she said, and grabbed another potato. "Ryan, when you run a company you feel responsible for the employees. Everything about the employees. If two of my people were injured in a fire in *my* building, I'd go."

As if absorbing that information Ryan didn't say anything for a minute, then he sighed and said, "I suppose I understood that part. What I didn't understand was that she had to get back to her office."

"Crisis control," Grace said simply. "Or crisis management."

"She has a staff."

"All of whom have jobs, I'm sure," Grace agreed amicably. "But Madison's the leader." She stopped, waited until she caught Ryan's gaze. "And whether you understand it or not, they need her."

"And whether you or Madison understand it or not, a whole carload of people tried to kill her two weeks ago. Who's to say that fire wasn't set to draw her out of hiding?"

Grace considered that for a second. "No one, I guess."

"Yet she ran off without a thought for anything except her companies."

Grace shook her head. "You're wrong, Ryan. When Madison left, she wasn't thinking about her company, she was thinking about her employees. They needed her."

"And Lacy didn't?"

"I don't honestly think this is about Lacy," Grace ventured softly. "Do you want to tell me what this is really about?"

Ryan closed his eyes. "It doesn't work, Grace. She told me two days ago that she was going to change her life, to make some time in her life so she could have a real relationship, but she can't. Her life doesn't let her. This problem only proves what I told her all along. A relationship between us would never work."

When Ryan grabbed another potato, Grace stopped him. "Ryan, whether you know it or not, you made it work. You're caring for Lacy so that Madison can do the right thing for her workers and her company. Thousands of employees would lose their jobs if Madison decided to close her company. Those are people, too. And all those people have families and kids. I think what Madison did was unselfish. I think what *you* did was unselfish."

"I think what I did was my job," Ryan said, tossing his potato into the water bowl. He grabbed a dish towel and wiped his hands. "I protected the baby I was assigned to protect. Nothing more. Nothing less. And if you think Madison did any more than protect her interests, then you're wrong on that, too,'' He walked to the kitchen door. ''I think I'll go see if Cal and Angus need any help.''

Chapter Sixteen

Unfortunately, Madison agreed with Ryan. As her temporary escort drove her to Angus's ranch later that afternoon, she thought about everything that had happened since she'd learned of the fire, and by the time they pulled onto the dusty lane that led to Angus's house, she conceded the same point Ryan had. Their relationship was doomed. Not because of the fire, or even because she went back to work, but because of how she handled Lacy.

She didn't put Lacy second. She always took care of Lacy, made provisions for Lacy—first—before she did whatever it was she had to do. But Ryan hadn't seen it that way. His interpretation of the situation was that Madison had gotten Lacy out of the way so she could take care of business.

Worse, and what troubled her now, was that he would never see that she'd taken care of Lacy, not gotten rid of her. His own life experience left him so cynical he'd *never* give Madison the benefit of the doubt. Every time she had a crisis and was forced to take extreme measures, Ryan would distrust her motives. He'd never see her putting her child first—or even putting him first—by ensuring that he and Lacy would be okay while she was gone. He would only see that she was going.

It hurt her to have him storm off with Lacy the night before, but it would kill her if their relationship went any further and he left her some night because he refused to understand the difference between obligation and selfishness.

As the car stopped in front of the ranch house, Madison took a long breath. She already loved him. She'd admitted that to herself long ago. Her heart would splinter into a million pieces when she left him. Yet she knew things weren't going to get better. If she didn't get out of this now, if she let herself grow closer, love him more, depend on him for emotions that right now were simply pleasant hopes, then leaving him would kill her.

And one thing was certain. She would leave him or he would leave her. They were not the kind of people who could live together. Love together, yes. Need each other, yes. But not live together.

Gathering her courage, she said goodbye to her escort, opened her car door and got out. She hadn't fully climbed the steps before Grace met her. "I'm glad you came," she said, linking her arm with Madison's. "I have a big pot of stew brewing, and I think it's about time for Lacy to get up from her nap."

Madison smiled appreciatively, but before she could say anything, Grace said, "Lacy's in Ryan's room. Third door on the right. You can get Lacy and wash up before dinner in whatever order seems appropriate."

At that Madison laughed. "Lacy hasn't been any trouble, has she?"

"She's a perfect child," Ryan said from behind her. "She hasn't been any trouble, and we've been happy to keep her."

He stayed in the foyer long enough to say his piece, then he strode past Grace and Madison and into the kitchen.

"He doesn't seem very happy to see me," Madison said, realizing that what she'd decided in the car was true.

"He needs a minute to get adjusted," Grace said reassuringly as she patted Madison's hand. "Go upstairs and get yourself and Lacy ready for dinner."

Madison smiled. "Okay," she said and started up the two-tiered staircase. She would make one last-ditch effort to bring Ryan around. She could give him her news that the fire wasn't arson, but simply an electrical malfunction. If she was wrong, if he wasn't annoyed that she'd put her business first, but was only angry because he felt she'd put her life in jeopardy, then this news should at least comfort him into realizing there was nothing to worry about.

She waited until everyone had an opportunity to grow accustomed to having Lacy at their table, albeit in her high chair. Then she waited until everyone told their favorite story of Lacy's visit. Then she waited while Angus and Cal discussed something about cattle. Then she waited while Grace told a story about her business. Finally, when it seemed as if everyone was waiting for her to tell her news, Madison cleared her throat and said, "We got preliminary results from the fire marshal today."

"This quickly?" Cal asked skeptically.

Noticing that Ryan's ears perked up even if he didn't speak, Madison nodded. "The results came in quickly since the origin of the fire was obvious. The fire wasn't arson," she said, "but the result of a short in an electrical panel."

"Really?" Angus said, filling in the silence that resulted because everyone was waiting for Ryan to comment.

Madison swallowed, then jumped in with both feet, hoping Ryan had merely missed the significance of what she'd said. "The people against whom I'm testifying hadn't set the fire to bring me out of hiding," she said encouragingly. "I'm perfectly safe."

"Well, that's a relief," Grace said, butting in before Angus could and since Ryan wouldn't. "I had a feeling everything was going to turn out all right. I'm glad to see it has." She paused, then kicked Ryan under the table. "Aren't you, Ryan?" she asked sweetly.

"Of course I am," he said quietly. "I was as worried as anybody else."

The conversation died again and Madison's heart sunk. So, she'd been right. He wasn't as concerned for her safety as he had been upset about the fact that he thought she put her company first. Knowing his past, she supposed she couldn't blame him.

"Who's ready for dessert?" Grace asked brightly, attempting to override the pained silence.

Ryan tossed his napkin beside his dish. "I'm not feeling very hungry right now," he said, then rose from his seat. "I think I'll go sit on the porch swing. You guys go on without me."

He left while everyone was still a little too shocked to stop him. When he was gone, Grace rose. "I'll bring the cake in here."

"I'll help you," Cal announced suddenly, bouncing from his chair.

Madison closed her eyes. The last thing she wanted was to drag Ryan's entire family into their dispute, yet that's exactly what had happened.

"We've faced a crisis a time or two in our lifetimes, you know," Angus said, breaking the silence after Cal and Grace left the room.

"I know," Madison said, opening her eyes. "I'm just embarrassed that you have to watch us behaving like children."

"You're not behaving like children. You're behaving like people who don't understand each other," Angus corrected, patting her hand. "Why don't you go out and talk to him. The kids and I will care for Lacy."

Madison sighed. "I suppose you're right."

"Of course, I'm right," Angus said, sounding like he couldn't believe she'd consider doubting him.

She found Ryan exactly where he said he would be: on the wide swing of the front porch. The screen door creaked as she pushed it and slid through the opening. "Can I join you for a second?"

"Sure. Why not? I'm guessing Angus told you to come out here and resolve this problem, so, sure, have a seat."

Uncomfortable, Madison sat beside him on the soft cushion that lay on the bench seat of the wooden swing. "You don't have to sound so sarcastic about the fact that Angus cares enough about you to want me to come out and resolve this."

"Resolve this?" Ryan shot back, pivoting to face her. "There's nothing to resolve. Things between us might have been iffy before, but your feelings tonight were patently clear."

Confused, Madison looked at him. "I have no idea what you're talking about."

"Oh, yeah? Then explain the purpose of announcing to everyone that I had been wrong about the arson. Were you rubbing it in? Or were you trying to make sure that—thickheaded as I can be—*I* recognized you were right and I was wrong?"

"I wasn't trying to make sure you knew I was right," Madison said with a gasp. "I was trying to make sure you knew I was safe."

"No, you weren't, Madison," Ryan angrily insisted. "You were trying to make sure that I knew you were right. Not so much because you wanted to be right," he added a little more calmly, "but because you wanted me to see that your instincts are correct when it comes to your business, in order that I wouldn't question you anymore."

Madison started to argue, then realized in a roundabout way he was right and she snapped her mouth closed.

"We're never going to come to an understanding about the way you work," he said, then rubbed his hand down his face. "I'm never, ever going to understand the way you live."

"No, I suppose you're not," Madison agreed quietly. She felt her heart being ripped in two. One half knew she had a commitment to the business she had started, to the people she employed, to the children for whom she would create in the future. The other half wanted a commitment to him. She wanted a commitment from him. But right at this moment she knew that wasn't going to happen.

"If you're telling me to leave, Ryan, I'll understand."

"I never said that."

"Well, I think what you are saying, or maybe what you're afraid to say, is that I'm not going to be able to keep the promises I made to you at the cabin."

"It's crossed my mind," he admitted softly.

She closed her eyes. Drew in a deep breath. "I don't think it's a good idea for us to see each other after the trial."

For a long moment there was nothing but night sounds. Then the swing creaked, and Madison felt the shift of weight that indicated that Ryan had risen from his seat.

"I'll go you one better," he said, starting for the door. "I'll get another police escort to take you to the trial, since you're so sure you're safe. Then we won't have to see each other again at all."

Nothing he said could have hurt her more. Stunned, feeling as if the breath had been knocked out of her, Madison glanced over at him. He opened the screen door, then paused and faced her again.

"You know, Madison, your company isn't going to keep you warm at nights."

Her eyes pleaded with him. "I can't give up everything I have, everything I am just because *you're* afraid."

"That's exactly why I'm letting you go."

He walked through the open door and out of her life, and Madison felt a shift as if her fate had been sealed.

Chapter Seventeen

Though Madison didn't see hide nor hair of Ryan, they spent the next day at the ranch together. She wasn't surprised he chose to sleep in the bunkhouse. She also wasn't surprised when, true to his word, Ryan arranged for another officer to escort Madison to the courthouse. Feeling oddly confused, she stood beside the police car, not quite sure what to do next.

"We'll keep Lacy until we get word from Jessica to bring her wherever you want her," Angus said, opening the passenger door for Madison. Beside him, Cal held a squirming Lacy. "You take care of yourself this morning, and we'll be here for you when you need us."

It was evident from what he said that Angus still had his apprehensions about this trial. Judging by the expression on Cal's face, Madison could see Cal wasn't as comfortable or as calm as he usually was. When Grace left the night before, she had also expressed her concerns. Madison still had a few doubts of her own. But obviously Ryan didn't feel the same way. Not only had he left her in the hands of a stranger for the second time, but he wasn't going to say goodbye. That hurt. It hurt more than Madison had thought possible.

But there was nothing she could do about Ryan or the way he felt. Nothing she could do about his mood swings or his here-today-gone-tomorrow feelings for her. Standing in the heat of the morning sun, she oriented herself to reality. Ryan didn't love her. He didn't even care about her. That was reality. That was what she had to deal with.

"Okay," Madison said, smiling at Angus before stepping into the car. "I'll make sure Jessica gives you a call."

Angus slammed the door. Cal helped Lacy wave goodbye. Madison blew her daughter a kiss, and then she was off. On her way to the courthouse. For all her big talk the past two weeks, suddenly she was scared. More frightened than she'd ever been in her entire life.

Keeping her eyes straight ahead, she concentrated on work, because work was all she had right now. Exactly as Ryan had warned her, she didn't have a life. She didn't have anything. Eyes straight ahead, she focused on children, on laughter, on making the world a better place. That was her calling. *That* was her life.

She didn't see Ryan's Bronco pull out of the bushes about a quarter mile behind the car in which she rode. She didn't see, because Ryan didn't want her to see. He'd said what he'd said in anger. And though he would be forced not to see her after the trial, since that's what she wanted, he refused to abdicate his position as her protector until she was safe.

So he followed her into town, followed her into the private parking garage in the basement of the courthouse, followed discreetly behind as she got into the elevator, then ran up the steps until he reached the floor housing the district attorney's offices. He watched as Jim Benson guided Madison into Jessica's suite. He watched the door close behind her, then he leaned against the cool wall. That was it. His job was done. He never had to see her again.

Squeezing his eyes shut, he fought to control the rush of emotion that nearly overwhelmed him.

He should be relieved.

In a sense part of this flood of feelings *was* relief. Guarding someone was never easy. Protecting someone as well-known as Madison had been next to impossible. It was always a comfort to finish a project like this.

So why the hell did he feel so damn bad?

Jessica rose from the chair behind her worn desk as Madison entered the room. "Good morning," she said cheerfully, grasping Madison's hands in welcome. "Jim, you can leave us now."

Jim Benson, the escort assigned to Madison in Ryan's stead, did exactly as he was told. Madison quickly faced Jessica. "What's happened?" she asked nervously. "I can tell something's happened."

"Something wonderful's happened," Jessica said, motioning for Madison to sit on the chair in front of her desk. "Your gang of crooks has turned state's evidence."

"What?" Madison asked, confused. "Against whom?"

"It seems they've been working for someone much more interesting than themselves. I had my staff investigating day and night for the past thirty-six hours, and all the information they gave us in their confessions has been verified."

"You're kidding?"

Jessica smiled. "Nope. Not only are you off the hook for the trial, but you're off the hook period. You have become irrelevant. You can go home now."

"Home?" Madison said as if the word were foreign.

Jessica laughed. "Yes, home. I'll call you tonight and fill you in. Right now I have a million details to attend to."

Madison rose slowly, as if not quite sure what to do. Jessica had already put her attention to some paperwork on her desk. Feeling disoriented, Madison left the office and walked into the huge domed foyer of the courthouse. She glanced at the spiral staircase, listened to the empty, hollow sound of footsteps, felt the coolness of the impersonal lobby.

For the first time in her entire life she felt alone.

Completely, absolutely, totally alone.

Work always gave Madison a sense of worth and perspective. She reminded herself of this as she waited for one of Jessica's staff to drive her to her office in Crossroads Creek. She might feel alone, but the truth of the matter was she hadn't made any wrong choices. Even if she had begged Ryan to understand her decisions about the fire, he wouldn't have backed down. He would have demanded the kind of compromise she couldn't make.

But that didn't mean she hadn't learned a lesson or two in that cabin in the woods. The minute she arrived in her office, she called her administrative staff in and announced that she was putting in a day care center.

"The cost is prohibitive," Max Ringer, her comptroller, announced immediately.

"I'm not concerned about the cost," Madison countered, then took a long, slow breath. "*I* want a day care center here. *I* want to be able to visit *my* child," she said, then watched as everyone's faces scrunched up in confusion. "I have a daughter," she continued, rising as everyone's mouth dropped open. "Up to this point I've kept her something of a secret because I wanted to protect her. Now, I see that was wrong. I want more time with her than I've had over the past year. So, I'm putting in a day care center. I want employees to feel comfortable to walk down to see their kids at any point in their day. I want the employees to eat lunch with their kids. I want kids to be first."

"That's going to be one hell of an expense," Max reiterated, shaking his head. "The company's not just bearing the cost of the rooms and day care workers, but we also have the cost of employee downtime."

"Hang the cost," Madison said with a laugh. "Max, we are a company that makes baby clothes, toys and furniture. Not putting kids first could be seen as bad for our image."

"It's still going to be expensive."

"Well, then I have something that will probably make your day. While I was away I came up with plans for a new line of matching dishes and linens. They'll include adult and child-size dinnerware and napkins made with bold bright designs to please kids. It will be something to bring adults together with kids at mealtime. I haven't worked out all the bugs yet, but when I do, it will be a gold mine. I can feel it."

Max smiled and shook his head again as if mildly exasperated. "So can I. Somehow or other you'll work this until it becomes the trend of the century."

Confident that she had the support of her employees, Madison pushed herself away from her desk to walk back to her chair. When she did she saw Ryan standing in her doorway, and her heart felt as if it had stopped. "Ryan?" she said, confused not merely because he was here but also because he must have gotten past her secretary. "What are you doing here?"

Ryan looked at the employees she had clustered in front of her desk, then at Madison. From that one glance, Madison could tell that he wouldn't be comfortable discussing whatever he'd come to discuss in front of her staff. From the wide-eyed expressions on their faces, Madison didn't blame him. First she'd disappeared for two weeks. Then she announced she had a child. Now a strange man—a tall, handsome, rugged-looking sheriff—stood in her doorway, Stetson in his hand.

"That's all we needed to discuss," she told her gawking employees as she briskly walked around her desk to her chair. "You can go...and close the door behind you," she added, then paused for a heartbeat. "Ryan, please come in."

It took about fifteen seconds for the exchange to be made. Her curious crew couldn't leave without checking out the man in her doorway, and Ryan couldn't enter until they left. When the last employee was gone and the door firmly closed behind him, Madison smiled cautiously. "Please, have a seat."

Ryan shook his head. "No," he said, glancing around her huge office, obviously taking in the black leather and chrome furniture, her glass desktop, the wall of windows behind her. The expression on his face became guarded. "What I have to say won't take long. Angus asked me to come here to invite you and Lacy to a barbecue."

Her heart plummeted. "I see."

"He got very attached to you both," Ryan explained, uncomfortably roaming the room. "I don't think he could handle having you leave as suddenly as you did this morning."

"Things got even more confusing after I got to the courthouse," Madison began, then realized Ryan would know by now that the people against whom she was to testify had turned state's evidence. Telling him this wouldn't be giving information, it would be confiding her feelings and he didn't want to hear about her feelings. That part of their relationship was over, gone. She couldn't bend. He *wouldn't* bend.

And she couldn't imagine spending two or three or four hours together at a party pretending she didn't love him. She couldn't imagine watching him talk with other people without trying to wedge her way into his conversations. She couldn't imagine not making a fool of herself vying for his attention.

"Give Angus my regrets," she said, then pretended great interest in some papers on her desk. "But Lacy and I won't be able to attend."

Ryan stopped pacing and just stared at her. Half of him wanted to argue, since Angus said he needed the extra time with Madison and Lacy to get accustomed to not having them in his life anymore. The other half knew that a quick break was better for him.

Madison sighed, glanced up from her paperwork. "Ryan, I'm afraid I'm going to have to ask you to leave. I have work to do."

Ryan nearly said, "I should have guessed," but he quickly stopped himself. He'd heard everything she said about the improvements she was making to her company. A strange sense of something almost like pride rose up in him. He knew beyond a shadow of a doubt that their time together had changed her. But he knew, too, that even in the beginning she hadn't been as bad as his parents…which also sort of wasn't true. Being with Madison had shown him that his parents had loved him in their own way. They certainly weren't Ward and June Cleaver, but they'd loved him. It took meeting Madison, seeing her with her child, and now seeing her in her work place, for him to recognize that.

Realizing that he was standing silently in the center of her office while she worked feverishly, Ryan scrubbed his hand over his mouth. There was nothing left to say. Nothing left to do. He turned and walked to her office door. He grabbed the knob and twisted it, but before he walked out, he took one *last* look at Madison because he knew it would be exactly that, his last look. Their paths would never cross again.

Chapter Eighteen

Madison issued a press release announcing the addition of the day care centers at her offices. It appeared in the next day's edition of the *Crossroads Creek Chronicle,* along with a picture of Madison holding Lacy. Ryan's heart lurched. He'd never seen anybody look so good to him. He told himself he'd known the woman a mere two weeks. He told himself that wasn't long enough to love someone. Yet every time he glanced at that picture, his heart hurt.

Determined to counter this rush of unwarranted feelings with pure, plain, perfect logic, Ryan dressed for work and walked from his apartment to the municipal building.

"Oooh-ee," Annabelle Parker exclaimed the minute he walked through the door. "Did you see that Delaney woman in the paper this morning?" she asked, her eyes round and luminous with excitement. "Not only is she changing her companies since that big fire, but she's got a daughter. Did you know that when you were guarding her?"

Ryan tossed his Stetson to an available peg. "Lacy was with us at Angus's cabin."

"Ooooh-eee!" Annabelle exclaimed. "You gotta give me the dirt on this one."

"There is no dirt," Ryan told the dispatcher. "This is the nineties, Annabelle. Why don't you step out of the Dark Ages and join the rest of us."

Annabelle gasped and clutched her chest. "I didn't mean to imply anything...."

"Then why don't we let Madison Delaney alone."

"Whatever you say, chief," Annabelle muttered and went back to reading her magazine.

Ryan ran his hand down his face. If he hadn't understood what Madison had been trying to tell him about her privacy, Annabelle had certainly cleared it up for him. Though Crossroads Creek was a small town and the residents tended to take care of one another, as kind as their intentions could typically be, they were, after all, only human. And if they were reacting this way, Ryan couldn't begin to imagine how her business associates were reacting this morning.

He blew his breath out on a long sigh. That was not his concern. He managed to occupy himself with paperwork and telephone calls until about eleven, when the walls of the building seemed to close in on him.

"I think I'll take a drive around town," Ryan decided, rising from his old wooden desk. He loved the municipal building. He loved his job. He even didn't mind paperwork. But his patience had about a three-hour limit normally. Worrying about Madison, a woman who obviously didn't need to be worried about, had his patience worn so thin he knew he needed a break right this minute.

He drew his Stetson from the peg by the door and walked out into the intense Texas sun. Though the streets were all paved and parking meters dotted the sidewalks, Ryan could imagine this town as it had been a hundred years ago, mostly because it hadn't grown much since its inception.

Crossroads Creek existed purely to supply the needs of the surrounding ranches.

He looked to the east, toward the big glass structure that stood out like a sore thumb. Madison's corporate office was the only modern building within a hundred miles. Even Grace's office was on the second floor of the bank, a bank that had been around for at least a century. Then Madison came along and put in a glass monstrosity to house her corporation. She hired everyone within a fifty-mile radius and when that wasn't adequate accountants and computer whiz kids to satisfy her needs, she imported more. Thanks to her, Crossroads Creek had a suburb, a small development that took up the west corner of Hank Hughes's ranch. Thanks to her suburb he'd been forced to hire a deputy, just to keep up with things.

He shook his head. She brought trouble. She brought change. Ryan was right to stay away from her.

He agreed with that logic until his drive took him parallel to the park. He saw her yellow hair first. How could anyone miss it? Then he realized she was wearing jeans and a faded sweatshirt and that Lacy was toddling on the sidewalk in front of the bench on which Madison sat.

He almost wrecked the car.

Damn her! What the hell was this supposed to be? It was Tuesday, she was supposed to be working.

He drove the cruiser away from the park as quickly as he could, but the next day at around lunchtime he couldn't help but cruise through the park one more time. And, sure enough, there she was. Sitting in the park, on a Wednesday, with her baby.

For twenty minutes he sat in his car watching her. But in the end he always came back to the same conclusion.

When the chips were down, she made her choice.

And it wasn't him.

It wasn't even Lacy.

Exhausted, drained, Ryan returned to the ranch on Saturday morning. Having worked two weeks straight guarding Madison, then finishing his shift at the municipal building, he was more than entitled to a little time off, and he intended to take it. What he needed right now was two weeks of working on the ranch—helping Cal—to empty his mind by burying himself in hard labor.

He jogged up the steps to the front door and let himself in the house. The second he entered the foyer, he heard Angus's booming voice. "What do you mean, you *can't* go?" Angus demanded angrily.

"I have two audits, remember?" Grace calmly replied. But though her voice wasn't strained, all of Ryan's senses went on red alert. Grace didn't get angry, rarely raised her voice. So her calm reply didn't mean she wasn't as irritated as her adopted father.

There was nothing worse for this family than a fight between Angus and Grace. When at all possible, Cal or Ryan intervened to prevent it. Out of habit, more than thought, Ryan turned and strode down the hall to the library where Angus lounged in his worn office chair, and Grace sat prim and proper in the chair across from his desk.

"Go after your audits, then."

Grace gasped. "That will be November! You want me to go to the mountains of Pennsylvania in November? They'll probably be buried under two feet of snow."

"I thought you liked snow."

"The kind we get here," Grace said. "Not the kind they get in Pennsylvania."

"What's the difference between—" Angus began but seeing Ryan in the doorway he stopped. "Come in, come in, boy. How'd it go?"

Ryan didn't need to ask Angus what his question meant. He knew exactly what Angus was talking about. In fact, it surprised Ryan that Angus hadn't called and asked long before this.

"She refused to come to the barbecue," Ryan said, and realized for the first time that that bothered him. Not only was any request from Angus special, and to be treated as such, but Ryan got a strange pang in the pit of his stomach. He knew it was over. He knew he and Madison weren't good for each other. Yet it hurt like the devil to realize she really was out of his life.

Angus leaned back in his chair, shrewdly assessed the situation, then slowly asked, "That's all?"

"Yes, that's all," Ryan barked, annoyed when he realized that he'd fallen into one of Angus's traps. Angus hadn't sent him to invite Madison to a barbecue, he'd sent Ryan to Madison's office to give them another chance to talk. The fact that it hadn't done any good caused Ryan to feel all the more angry, all the more confused. How could he want someone so much who was so bad for him?

"How can you let her get away?" Angus asked angrily. "Never in your entire life have you made cow eyes at a woman. I always figured the first time you did, that woman would have to be very special. And she is. Yet you're standing here telling me that you're going to let her get away."

"She's not right for me and I'm not right for her, Angus," Ryan said tranquilly enough, though inside, his guts were twisting. Angus was right. He knew Angus was right. But he also knew Angus was wrong. Ryan might care for Madison. She might care for him, but they were wrong for each other. Dead wrong.

"And that's it?"

"That's it."

Frustrated, Angus tossed his papers to his desk and sprang from his seat. "You're an idiot," he sputtered, rounding his desk. "A pure, unadulterated idiot," he added, heading for the door. "I'm going for a glass of water."

When the door slammed behind him, Grace leaned back in her chair. "Ten to one he's going for Scotch."

Taking the chair beside hers, Ryan said, "You think he's that angry with me?"

"I think it's a combination of the two of us. He's the silent partner in a ski resort in Pennsylvania, but the place isn't making any money. He wants me to go and check it out."

"Why don't you?"

Grace shook her head. "Because I not only have tons of work to keep me busy for the next several months, but I also have an odd feeling about this. It's almost like a warning of sorts not to go."

"That's funny, I had an odd feeling about guarding Madison."

"How's that?"

He shook his head. "I can't explain it except to say it was kind of like destiny was dragging me into something that I didn't want to do."

"That's exactly the feeling I have now," Grace said, then gently tapped the back of the hand he had resting on the arm of his chair. "Except we've both seen Angus's business partners, and I don't think I have to worry about falling in love with one of them."

Ryan laughed in spite of himself. "You can make jokes all you want, but I don't want to talk about this."

"Of course you don't," Grace agreed cheerfully. "No one wants to admit they were kicked out of someone's office."

"She didn't kick me out of her office."

"Really? Then what did happen?"

Sighing as if admitting defeat, Ryan glanced over at Grace. "I'm not entirely sure. I walked in on a meeting where she was explaining to her people that things were going to change somewhat at her company, and just as smooth as you please she added that she had a daughter."

"Yikes," Graces said, again patting his hand. "That must have been difficult."

He shook his head. "It wasn't difficult as much as it was confusing. I knew she wanted to change, but I didn't think that she could."

"And now that she has?" Grace prompted.

He shrugged. "I don't know. I want to trust her." He squeezed his eyes shut. "God, I want it more than I ever believed I could want anything, but I can't."

"Have you tried?"

That opened his eyes. For a few seconds he stared at Grace. She took both his hands in hers. "I know that you're scared because of your past," she said. "I'm scared, too. Angus didn't merely save you from a life of loneliness. He also saved me and Cal. So I know exactly what you're going through. I'm not sure I'll ever find the right man, and when I do, I'm not sure I'll be able to trust him enough to give my heart. But that doesn't mean I'm not going to try."

"I tried," Ryan said, though he knew that wasn't true. He'd fought falling in love every step of the way.

"Then I guess what you're really telling me is that you've given up. You've found what you want but you refuse to go after it." She shook her head. "I never thought I'd see the day *you'd* be a coward."

"I'm not a coward," Ryan argued, but he got the twisting feeling in his guts again. He'd never been afraid of anything. Nothing, damn it! And he wasn't afraid of this.

Grace slowly rose from her chair. "I think I'll go join Angus for a glass of water."

Grace closed the door behind her, and Ryan found himself sitting alone in Angus's den. He heard the distant sound of the grandfather clock in the front hall as it chimed out the hour, but otherwise the world was silent.

And he knew that was the sound of the rest of his life. The cold, empty sound of nothing.

At eight o'clock that night, Madison opened her front door to find Ryan standing on the threshold, dressed in his usual worn jeans, chambray shirt and cowboy hat.

For a few stunned seconds she simply stared at him, then he grabbed her around the waist, hauled her against him and pressed his lips to hers. For Madison the world spun. She longed to wrap her arms around him, longed to let him hold her and kiss her for as long as he wanted. Everything inside of her yearned for the things that only he could give her. Everything inside of her wanted him and only him.

But common sense warred with instinct. He'd kissed her before. He'd come damned close to telling her he loved her. Yet he had still walked out on her, walked away from her when she needed him the most.

Ryan broke the kiss and rested his forehead on hers. Madison used that time to get her bearings, preparing to ask him to leave, but before she could open her mouth, Ryan said, "Madison, I love you."

Stunned, she pulled away.

"I wanted to tell you all along, almost from the first day I met you, but I was afraid."

"Afraid?"

"Yeah," he said, his lips bowing upward slightly into a self-deprecating smile. "I was afraid."

"Okay, I think I understand that," Madison said cautiously as she stepped away from him, needing to put some distance between them so her instincts wouldn't make a commitment she couldn't keep. He seemed to take it as a sign that she'd invited him in, and he stepped into her all-white foyer and closed the beveled glass door behind him.

Though she hadn't invited him in, what she had to say to him was better said privately than on her front porch. Drawing in a long, life-sustaining breath, she faced him again. "I understand, but I can't handle your going back and forth between loving me and not loving me, because whether you recognize it or not, that's what you've been doing all along.''

Hat in his hands, Ryan said, ''I know.''

Realizing she hadn't made her point, she sighed heavily. ''I know you know, but what I'm telling you is that knowing what you've been doing isn't good enough. You have to make a commitment and stick to it, and I'm not sure you can. Marrying me means more than a wife, kids and a white picket fence. Sometimes it will mean fund-raisers, charities, late-night board meetings. The man I marry has to be there for me. Publicly and privately. It won't work unless you understand that.''

Ryan drew in a long breath. ''I understand that. I understand it better than I ever thought I could.'' He paused, drew in another breath. ''In fact, I'm thinking about calling my parents.''

Madison took a step back. ''What?''

''I'm thinking about calling my parents,'' he said, rolling the brim of his hat between his nervous fingers. ''You made me see things in a way I never had before. You made me realize that maybe my parents felt they had a gift, too.'' He paused and sighed heavily. ''And you made me see that maybe my parents didn't intend to leave me alone as much as they intended accomplish some very worthwhile goals.'' He caught her gaze. ''They employ a good many people, too.''

She nodded. ''I guess they do.''

''And I sort of considered my own part in things.''

Her eyes widened in curiosity, but she didn't say anything.

''I have to wonder if I didn't make things worse by being rebellious.''

''It's a possibility.''

''I want to give us all a second chance. Me and my parents. But I want to do more than start over. I want to get it right this time. I don't want to jump to conclusions or walk away when things don't go the way I think they should. I want to work on our relationship until everything goes the best it can. I guess I finally realized we all have to compromise.''

She was completely silent for a full ten seconds, then, after licking her dry lips, Madison said, "It sounds like you've thought this all through."

"You were that important to me."

Tears gathered in the corners of her eyes. "*I* was that important to you?"

"You were. After only two weeks, and two weeks of following you for twelve hours a day before the episode in the parking garage, I realized I couldn't live without you. No," he amended, shaking his head. "I realized I didn't *want* to live without you, but I knew I'd never come to terms with your life unless I tried to put my parents' lives in perspective, too. And I have."

"I don't know what to say."

"You could tell me that you love me."

Madison swallowed hard. "I don't merely love you, I adore you."

He grinned wickedly and pulled her into his arms. "You don't have to go that far."

"Yes, I do. What you did for me was absolutely amazing."

He shook his head. "I'm a very selfish man. I didn't do it for you, I did it for me."

Pulling back so she could look at him, Madison said, "Maybe you did it for us?"

He nodded. "I did it for us."

The sound of Lacy crying piped through the intercom system, and Madison drew back. "I'm being paged."

Ryan tossed his hat to a brass coat hook. "I'll do the honors."

"*You'll* get her?"

Ryan sent her a wounded expression. "I cared for her the entire time she stayed with Angus."

"She'll probably need to be changed," Madison warned carefully.

"And she needed to be changed while she was at the ranch, too. I can handle it, Madison."

"This I have to see."

"Bring your notebook, I'm very good. I might teach *you* something," Ryan said, slipping his arm around her shoulders as he guided her up the steps.

They returned downstairs twenty minutes later. Lacy had been bathed and put into pajamas, and Ryan read her a story before they both tucked her in.

Madison felt as if she were walking on a cloud. Nothing could make her life any better. When they entered her living room, Ryan pulled her into his arms and kissed her, and Madison gave herself up to the rush of emotion that overwhelmed her, thanking her lucky stars that something had pushed him into rethinking his decisions.

Curious, she drew away from him. "So, what did make you do all the soul searching you must have done this afternoon?"

Ryan put his arm around her shoulders and led her to an available sofa. "Let's just say it's not right for the sheriff of a small town to be a coward."

* * * * *

Take 4 bestselling love stories FREE
a FREE surprise gift!

Special Limited-time Offer

Mail to Silhouette Reader Service™

3010 Walden Avenue
P.O. Box 1867
Buffalo, N.Y. 14240-1867

YES! Please send me 4 free Silhouette Romance™ novels and my free surprise gift. Then send me 6 brand-new novels every month, which I will receive months before they appear in bookstores. Bill me at the low price of $2.90 each plus 25¢ delivery and applicable sales tax, if any.* That's the complete price and a savings of over 10% off the cover prices—quite a bargain! I understand that accepting the books and gift places me under no obligation ever to buy any books. I can always return a shipment and cancel at any time. Even if I never buy another book from Silhouette, the 4 free books and the surprise gift are mine to keep forever.

215 SEN CF2P

Name	(PLEASE PRINT)	
Address	Apt. No.	
City	State	Zip

This offer is limited to one order per household and not valid to present Silhouette Romance™ subscribers. *Terms and prices are subject to change without notice. Sales tax applicable in N.Y.

USROM-696 ©1990 Harlequin Enterprises Limited

ALICIA SCOTT

Continues the twelve-book series— 36 Hours—in March 1998 with Book Nine

PARTNERS IN CRIME

The storm was over, and Detective Jack Stryker finally had a prime suspect in Grand Springs' high-profile murder case. But beautiful Josie Reynolds wasn't about to admit to the crime— nor did Jack want her to. He believed in her innocence, and he teamed up with the alluring suspect to prove it. But was he playing it by the book—or merely blinded by love?

For Jack and Josie and *all* the residents of Grand Springs, Colorado, the storm-induced blackout was just the beginning of 36 Hours that changed *everything!* You won't want to miss a single book.

Available at your favorite retail outlet.

He's more than a man, he's one of our

Fabulous Fathers

Join Silhouette Romance as we present these heartwarming tales about wonderful men facing the challenges of fatherhood and love.

January 1998:
THE BILLIONAIRE'S BABY CHASE by Valerie Parv (SR#1270)
Billionaire daddy James Langford finds himself falling for Zoe Holden, the alluring foster mother of his long-lost daughter.

March 1998:
IN CARE OF THE SHERIFF by Susan Meier (SR#1283)
Sexy sheriff Ryan Kelly becomes a father-in-training when he is stranded with beautiful Madison Delaney and her adorable baby.

May 1998:
FALLING FOR A FATHER OF FOUR by Arlene James (SR#1295)
Overwhelmed single father Orren Ellis is soon humming the wedding march after hiring new nanny Mattie Kincaid.

Fall in love with our FABULOUS FATHERS!
And be sure to look for additional FABULOUS FATHERS titles
in the months to come.

Available at your favorite retail outlet.

Silhouette ROMANCE™

Return to the Towers!

In March
New York Times bestselling author

NORA ROBERTS

brings us to the Calhouns' fabulous
Maine coast mansion and reveals the
tragic secrets hidden there for generations.

For all his degrees, Professor Max Quartermain has a
lot to learn about love—and luscious Lilah Calhoun is
just the woman to teach him. Ex-cop Holt Bradford is
as prickly as a thornbush—until Suzanna Calhoun's
special touch makes love blossom in his heart.
And all of them are caught in the race to solve
the generations-old mystery of a priceless
lost necklace…and a timeless love.

Lilah and Suzanna
THE
Calhoun Women

A special 2-in-1 edition containing
FOR THE LOVE OF LILAH and
SUZANNA'S SURRENDER

Available at your favorite retail outlet.